THE HUNDRED MILLION BET

ATUL KOUL RANDEV

Srishti
Publishers & Distributors

Srishti Publishers & Distributors
A unit of AJR Publishing LLP
212A, Peacock Lane
Shahpur Jat, New Delhi – 110 049

editorial@srishtipublishers.com

First published by
Srishti Publishers & Distributors in 2023

10 9 8 7 6 5 4 3 2 1

This is a work of fiction. The characters, places, organisations and events described in this book are either a work of the author's imagination or have been used fictitiously. Any resemblance to people, living or dead, places, events, communities or organisations is purely coincidental.

Printed and bound in India

For Mom, for bringing me closer to stories,
and for passing on the dream to write.

For Dad, for gifting me your indomitable spirit.
This one is yours.

Meet the Characters

Caesar & friends

Jules – Poker player
Sumer – Jules' friend and Poker companion
August– Jules' friend and Poker companion
Zara – Girl at the party
Octavia – Jules' sister

Amir's shack

Amir / Boy – Maurya's enforcer
Victoria – Amir's girlfriend
Agent – Boy's agent from an art gallery in Paris

Maurya and all his unfortunate friends

Maurya – Proprietor of Paradise City
Maya – Maurya's younger sister
Father – Maurya & Maya's father
Amita – Maurya's wife
Vishnu Gupta – Maurya's accountant and mentor
Dhanraj Nanda – Leader of the cartel in the north

The Don's entourage

Don Camorra – The man who loses a hundred million euros to Caesar
Mishka – Don's employee
Jenia – Don's employee and Mishka's twin brother

Other characters

Don and Donna Fichera – Farmer couple living in a beach town in Northwest of Italy
Birgitte – Bar owner

Excerpt from August's Diary

What Would it Take to Survive?

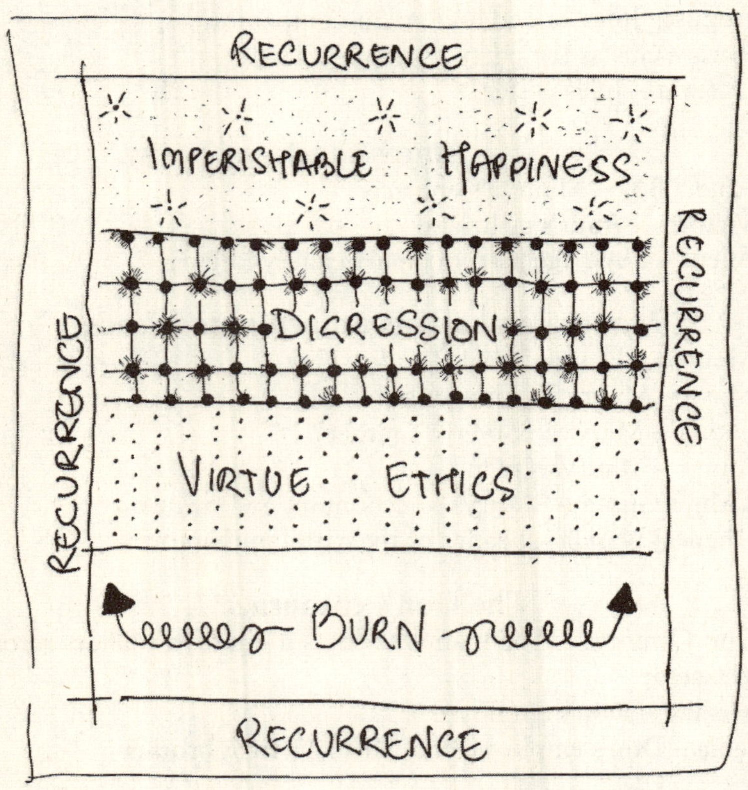

* Illustration by Anshika Koul.

Prologue

"How long have I known you?" Maurya asked Boy.

"Twenty years, give or take," Boy answered.

"I think it's about time that you told me your name."

They were on the rooftop of the Grand Hotel, looking out at the city that sprawled both upwards and outwards. A couple of hundred guests milled around the terrace; glamorously dressed patrons moved between a smattering of champagne towers.

"Paradise City, eh," Boy said instead. "You finally did it, building your own heaven on earth." He lifted his glass to drink, but stopped when he found it empty, "Could have been a little subtle with the name, but I guess it is a privilege of the maker."

Maurya laughed, "It is."

A tinge of grey had begun to colour Maurya's temple.

"It seems as if a couple of lifetimes have passed since we first met," Maurya said.

"They have," Boy smiled, "Yours and mine."

Maurya laughed again, "Touché." There was an easiness in his laughter that Boy had only begun to hear recently.

A waitress moved between them to collect Boy's empty glass. She was dressed in a white silk shirt that clung almost lustily to her torso; the short skirt had a slit across one thigh and managed to fit snugly around her derrière, and for a moment Boy wondered how it might feel to run his hand up her leg and under her skirt.

"You have come a long way, Maurya, from your relatively humble beginnings. Are you happy with what you've achieved?" he turned his attention back to Maurya.

"Moderately happy," Maurya answered.

Boy shook his head, "You are insatiable," he said. "What would make you truly happy?"

"Finding out your name."

"I only tell it to friends; you are not only my friend... you are also my boss."

"Does that mean you'll tell it to me the day you stop working for me?"

"Indeed."

Another waitress was back with a fresh drink in her hand, which she expertly deposited in front of Boy. He felt a violence stirring up inside him as he sensed her perfume when she leaned in close. Those buttons on her shirt did not look like they'd be able to withstand a strong tug; the skirt did not seem capable of putting up much resistance either for that matter. He would be willing to bet that it would take him less than ten seconds to get her out of those clothes, if she'd let him, of course. He looked up and saw that she had been staring at him.

"What's your name?" he asked her.

"Victoria," she said, "Yours?"

"Everyone calls me Boy."

She nodded and walked away.

"I should go," Boy said to Maurya. "I have an early start tomorrow."

"But the night is still young."

"And I have plans for it."

He laughed again. "Alright, leave me here, I'll just spend the evening looking at my gorgeous date." He turned his attention back to the glittering city. "She's promised that she'll stay here all night, for she is as insatiable as me."

Boy passed next to Victoria on his way out, a silky old man had his hand resting on her lower back, "I'll have a gin and tonic, honey."

"Anything else, sir?"

"You, if you'd like to join me for the evening."

"I'm afraid that's not on the menu," she said as she extricated herself from his grasp. A little venom sneaked into her eyes as the man coped an opportunistic pinch, but she did not let her smile waver, "I'll be right back with your drink."

Boy thought of that man's hand on Victoria as he drove towards the other end of the city. What would the old pervert have done had she agreed to go back with him for the night? He would probably have groped her all the way in the taxi to his hotel. He hardly looked like he was the gentle kind. He would have clumsily taken her clothes off, before sending her down to work on his limp dick. After a while he would have grabbed her by her gorgeous blonde hair and pushed her lithe body back on the bed. Her generous breasts would flop a little to the side as she opened her legs to accept him. He'd then climb in between her legs, lay his unwieldy body on top of her and push himself in.

That was not how Boy would treat her.

He sighed. He'd just have to go back tomorrow and see if he could rescue her from another night of butt pinching.

He pulled up in front of an apartment building and took the elevator to the top floor.

Maya opened the door, "You took your time getting here, Amir."

"Your brother wouldn't stop regaling about his beautiful city," he said.

She laughed, "He is in love again," she said as she stepped aside to let him in.

Book I

1
Caesar

Milano
August, 2015

"All in."

I was playing with a 3 and a 5. The table had a 6, a jack and a queen. Playing with me on the table were the owner of a popular car company, an artist who some called the best of his generation, a luxury clothing brand owner, and one of the most notorious Mafiosos this side of the Atlantic.

I was winning, or if you'd allow me the opportunity to rephrase, over the past few hours I had extracted twenty-five million euros from the small crowd. I suppose you wouldn't fault me for considering a quick exit. However, that is not what I did, and I can blame that on two things: first, at that point I thought I was playing the last game of my life, and hence this was my last chance to collect a large retirement bonus. Second, I was on the brink of succumbing to the animal instinct to continue playing while I was winning.

Fortunately for me, it was not just me who is occasionally taken over by the animal inside us. It is indeed a malady that haunts everyone, and once triggered, it'll make you do things that would seem unnatural at any other time. I had to carefully nurture, tease and draw out that animal towards that final round where they'd be willing to bet everything on the game.

"I'll go all in," I said.

This was met with blank stares from the others. "I'm out," said Giovanni.

"This is a disaster!" said Federico.

"You bastard!" said Emmanuelle. It wasn't the first expletive directed towards me that night.

Don Camorra played on. He looked at the dealer and then tapped the table to indicate that he would see the hand out.

We turned our cards on the table while the dealer flipped the *turn*. It was a 4. My heart must have stopped for a few seconds as the dealer paused before flipping the *river*. The 3 and the 5 in my hand longed to unite with the 4 and the 6 on the table. A 5-card sequence is a party in Poker, 4 cards are only good enough for what-ifs.

"Two. The full house wins."

The Don was out of money, the game was over, and I had pulled in a fifty million retirement bonus. The others gave me churlish glances while I slowly signed the dealer slip and added my bank details to the note.

"Are you leaving?" said Don Camorra as I began to get up.

"I can stay if you like, but I'm usually terrible company after a game." It was hard to maintain an air of self-reassurance on the outside when my mind was busy planning how I was going to spend my fortune.

"Do you want to play more?" he asked.

Go home to Victoria, my heart said. "Sure," my brain responded instead.

The others looked at the Don as he made a phone call to sanction the funds.

"May I have some whisky, please?" I asked a server.

"Are you sure you want to drink while you are in the middle of a game?"

"Very sure."

He nodded.

The dealer's phone beeped soon after.

"Don Camorra's credit has been granted."

This is a good moment to apprise you of three more facts. Fact number one: I do not understand how losing might feel, because I never lose. Nada. Nope. Never. I refuse. I have never walked away from a weekend of playing in my life with less money than I've entered-with.

Second, my name is Caesar. It is not the name I was born with, nor one that I was given. It was the name I took.

Third, I'm a man of very limited needs. But recently, I had come across a task that needed a sizeable investment. An investment along the lines of a hundred million euros, and here I was sitting at a table with just the right amount of money that I needed at stake.

The game that day brought back memories of *another night* from a long time ago; it was an important event that we should go back to at some point. But for now, let's stay in the present. I often forget the present. Is that something that happens to you too? I like to digress. It is perhaps the finest human skill, digression. Why arrive at something quickly when you can walk around in circles all day?

Don Camorra played like a man who wanted to win his money back. There were no subtle testing hands.

"Two pairs win," the dealer said. I lost a hand. The Don decided to go all in on a hand where the best I had was a king.

I managed to turn it around a little over the next few hands.

The dealer turned two kings on the *flop* along with a low card. I raised the bet; the *turn* had another king hiding behind it. The Don went all in again. Unfortunate as it was, he hadn't given the law of averages enough credit and this is the first lesson that I can pull out of the annals of my not so humble life – if you go all in over and over again, one of those hands will eventually end up going against you. And if that is how you play, then the only hand that matters is the last one.

On that particular life-defining hand, I had the fourth king. I flipped it on the table, threw what I then considered to be a respectful nod at my competitors and walked out before I could be persuaded to play again. Last game ever, I thought. It is almost morbidly *funny*, how wrong I was. Then again, life's morbidity is best expressed in humour; wait, make that humour and digression. Anyway, let's get started, for this is my story of loss, of gain, of one not-so-great escape, and of three rather unfortunate deaths.

2
Caesar

Milano
August, 2015

"Always enter a game with a plausible exit."

I had carried a plane ticket in my pocket all evening. I didn't have to, but when you are on your way to getting royally carried away in the heat of the moment with money going out and coming in, a slight cold tap on your pocket can bring you back to the present. As fortunate as it was, today it would help me make a quick exit.

I retrieved my wallet and phone from the security scanner and walked lazily through the stores at the airport.

The Don's people caught up with me while I stood in the queue to board the plane, "Mr Caesar, we'd like to have a chat with you."

"Is there a problem?"

"Indeed, this is about your luggage."

A few people were beginning to look at us, "There has to be some confusion. I'm travelling light and have no luggage."

"Mr Caesar, I must request you to come with us," the man said in a way that did not sound like a request at all.

A few minutes later, we were seated in a tiny, sparse room with little furniture. On the other side of the table sat a man from the Don's entourage, whom I had seen earlier in the evening.

"Good to see you again, Senor Caesar. How is life treating you?"

"I must admit, this minor inconvenience has become the cause of a slight headache, but apart from that, life has been fairly reasonable."

That man had been standing behind the Don all evening; he had a distinctively hooked nose and dark hair and spoke with as fine an Italian accent as any I'd ever heard. "I'm glad to hear that and I apologise for the inconvenience. Rest assured, if we have your full cooperation, this headache shall be quite short-lived." He paused. "I have something to show you," he said and flipped his phone towards me.

Up came the image of a girl with a rag binding her face. It took me a moment to recognise that the shell-shocked girl in the video was Octavia. An all too familiar bewildered sadness lined her tired face, as if she couldn't quite fathom why she was here, but something within her believed that she probably deserved it.

"As you can see, we have managed to secure custody of your sister. We can be efficient when we want to be. The kind lady, feisty, I might add, is safe and secure for now, and I must assure you that the condition will be maintained till the time that we have your kind cooperation."

"What, may I ask, am I to cooperate with?"

He sighed. "It is simple. We need you to come back to the game."

"You want me to give the money back?"

"No. We want you to play with it," he said, "till you lose."

The scream of the girl in the video cut through the silence that followed the man's words. "Why go through the ruse when we could end this right now?"

He sighed again. "Well Mr Caesar, there is a lot you need to learn. The Don is a proud man and does not like to take people's money from them; he likes to win it *fair and square*."

A part of me had believed that the Don would let me walk away with the money. I knew now, that it had been a stupid part of me.

"Quick question before I sign on the dotted line, what happens if I do not have the capacity or the will to cooperate?"

The man looked at the two men who had accompanied me to the room, "Such a situation, should it arise, would be to no one's benefit. You see, the amiable looking lady in the picture is bound to experience immense pain till the ordeal ends. As for yourself, I'd say that there is a certain level of risk attached to your kind person as well."

He continued, "Our friend Mishka over here is going to act like your personal escort, a bodyguard from this moment on. You will walk out of the door and get into a car with him without fuss. It should be a short trip. If you disregard this brief interchange, it might even be a pleasant trip." I looked at Mishka, who appeared to be anything but pleasant. "Have a good night's sleep in your hotel. But please remember to turn up at the given address tomorrow evening at eight p.m. sharp for the game. Once you are at the game, life should be relatively simple. Play as freely as you like. Remember that the longer the game lasts, the longer this ordeal stretches for all of us."

I looked down at the video. The terror was still fresh on her face; perhaps the reality of her captivity had not begun to sink in.

"All right," I said, mustering a neutral nod, and then walked out of the room.

3
Caesar

Road to Zurich
August, 2015

"Where are we going?" I asked Mishka. He chose not to respond.

We had driven straight into the heart of the mountains up north from Milano. The glittering Casino di Campioni sat lazily next to Lake Lugano on a tiny piece of Italy, surrounded from all sides by Switzerland.

"I once played with the son of the last king of Italy in that Casino," I said to Mishka. "He was an interesting character. At the age of sixty-five, he punched his sixty-one-year-old cousin in the face twice, gave him a bloody upper lip. I bet he would have done the same to me, had I not let him win."

I paused to read the flashing signs.

"Why?" I heard Mishka ask.

"What was that?"

"Why did you let him win?"

I paused to ponder, and then replied, "Big men with big egos. I know they hate losing. So I let him win one evening and he was happy for a day.

Mishka didn't respond, but I could tell that he was listening.

"He came out the next day to play me again. I let him win a second time."

"He wanted to play me a third time, and this time, I took him long into the game. I took him to the edge and kept him there, till he broke. Because you see, Mishka, it is not something in our control. No matter how much in control we think we are, we always snap in the end. Everyone has a limit."

I looked at Mishka, expecting to see glee, but came face to face with utter boredom. "Did he punch you in the face?"

"No."

"That's a bad story."

I suppressed my frustration. "You don't understand, my dear brute..."

"I understand, gambler... let Mishka drive in peace. Don't waste my time telling me stories where nobody gets punched in the face, or I will hit you and give your story a new ending. Then you can tell people that there was a time I was telling a story about the last king of Italy and then this guy punched me in the face. That'll be a good ending."

I almost readied a wisecrack, but the close confines of the car weren't made for sarcastic quips to be directed at a possibly psychotic murderer.

"It was the *son* of the last king of Italy," I clarified.

***

The only place where rational decision-making has a home is in the present, and yet we cling to the past for an inordinate amount of time. I searched for the canvases of my past to prop up my present and many memories of Octavia jumped up. One memorable weekend back from about fifteen years ago stood out.

My Parisian flatmates and I had been out on a playing trip and had decided to take a short detour to a friend's beach house in the south of France. Our luck had been running low after the first few days and we needed a break to clear our heads.

Octavia had driven ten hours the night before with a few girlfriends to spend the weekend with us. Sumer used the evening to impress the girls with his taco consumption skills while I rekindled my friendship with Don Julio.

Octavia was pretty; her strong chin and curly hair would make her stand out in any crowd, but she refused to give in to the base urge of seeking pleasure from appreciation of others. Her friends, on the other hand, moved around with the flirtatious energy of nineteen-year-olds who were used to getting attention.

It was the middle of the afternoon and we had tickets to a concert for that evening. A cruel irony must have been at play because in the few hours that we had to kill, we found ourselves at a *chupito* bar. Octavia wasn't drinking that evening because they didn't have any beer. The others, I might speak with some judgment here, while including myself in it all, were drinking as if it was going out of fashion.

It was after the fourth shot in four minutes that someone came up with the idea that we needed to time ourselves between shots if we wanted to have any chance of making it to the concert.

We were seven people, so someone suggested that we should do seven rounds with seven minutes each between them.

"Does that include the four shots we've already had?" Sumer asked.

"A most poignant question, I must admit," I said as I pondered over it in my drunken seriousness. "My proposal is that we only count the shots consumed hereafter."

I'll admit, it looked good till shot number five. Five counted after the aforementioned hereafter, the one that was now about twenty-eight minutes in the past. Things took a sudden turn for the worse when Sumer decided to empty his ill-consumed tacos on one of Octavia's friends. For some reason, that killed the vibe. The girls got into a fight with each other, and the guy who tried to intervene got punched in the neck, though that may have been the girl punching

Sumer for throwing up on her, it is hard to say. What I can say with certainty is that the crowd decided to go back to the little villa we were staying in for the weekend. The concert was forgotten.

"What's up with you?" Octavia asked as she sat down next to me on the front porch a short while later. I had been enjoying the cool summer breeze and inspecting the deep purple of the sky.

"Nothing..." I said, "something," I followed. I twirled one of the strands of her seemingly impossible curls around my finger to measure its resistance and it complied for a second before breaking free.

"The state of affairs for the evening have so distressed the company, that there seems to be no way to salvage the evening, and yet, when I take a step back and look at our problems objectively from the perspective of an impartial observer – it is a small problem.

"Even though, I'm equipped to look at it from that perspective and comment on its simplicity, I still cannot escape the feeling of personal despair at missing out on that concert."

Octavia had a kind expression on her face.

"Perhaps I need to practice it more," I said, "The art of observing things from the perspective of eternity. Baruch Spinoza had a name for it; he called it *sub specie aeternitatis*."

She looked at me for a moment, and then walked into the house.

"Hey, I didn't mean to bore you."

A few minutes later, she was back with a bottle of rum. "I bet Captain Morgan can help us lighten the mood and salvage the evening a wee bit?"

"You are a true member of your family," I said as I plucked the bottle out of her hand.

She moved closer to me and rested her head on my shoulder, "You cannot begrudge yourself for what you hold as a worry close to your heart," she said, "and in any case all problems are consequential– for the world is a sum total of all its problems, is it not?"

She pulled up to give me a quick kiss, then went back into a state of stupor.

"What's happening out here?" Sumer said, as he slid down next to us. "Rum. I want some rum."

He answered my look of scepticism with words of his own, "I've already emptied everything that was in my stomach. The problem were the tacos and not the alcohol; the alcohol, as you are about to see, is the cure."

While he convinced no one apart from himself, I passed the bottle to him anyway.

I continued to inspect the glorious purple of the clouds.

4
Caesar

Zurich
August, 2015

A note had been left behind at the dresser in my hotel room in Zurich with the address. I pulled out a small bottle of whisky from the mini bar and drank straight from it. What choices did I have?

I could lose the money and hope that they let Octavia and me walk away. But could I trust them to let her out? Did I really care? Should you feel inclined to question the basis of my dilemma, let me point out that a hundred million euros was a substantial amount of money. In addition, if you'll forgive my callousness for a moment, Octavia had, to the best of my estimates, lived a fairly ordinary life so far. A life that was unlikely to take even a modestly remarkable turn in the foreseeable future. In an exceedingly boring life that could at best be described as transient, this was probably the one life-altering event she had experienced. Would it be fair for me to deprive her of this turmoil?

She was trapped in a room. How different was it from her day-to-day existence? She couldn't move around in freedom, but trading it for the knowledge that the events that remained were both remarkable and finite seemed to be a fair trade to me. Not to mention the fact that it also meant that I might be able to keep my money.

Which brought me to my second alternative – run. The Don was unlikely to give up the chase for his money easily, but then again, the world was a big place, and that money could buy me a fair amount of space to lose myself in. How long would it take before they caught up with me? Five years? One? It was highly unlikely that I would go on to live long anyway, considering my current debauched lifestyle.

I arrived at the location of the game a few minutes before eight p.m. "Welcome Mr Caesar, it is a pleasure to receive a player of your stature at our modest establishment." An oily man welcomed me at the door. He led me into a room with large floor to ceiling windows that gazed outwards on a large body of water. A table was set up in the centre of the room for the game.

"It's my utmost pleasure to provide you with this privilege, my dear sir."

The man's fake smile widened even further. "Would you like something to drink before we start?"

"I'm fine, thank you." A placard with my name on it sat in front of the chair. An envelope rested next to it.

Inside the envelope was a picture of Octavia holding up the day's newspaper. It was pretty old school, as far as intimidation tactics went.

"What do you seek today, Mr Caesar?" The Don's voice rang out from behind. "You must excuse me for inconveniencing you for my indulgence."

They sought reactions that I was unwilling to give. 'Do not weep. Do not wax indignant. Understand', said Spinoza. Right now, that is what I'm seeking, Don Camorra. This is what I've been seeking for a few decades, so not much has changed. Just the perspective has shifted, now that another person has been brought into it."

The Don followed my gaze to the envelope with Octavia's picture in it, "What are you trying to understand?"

"Relationships today, and their value in my life."

The Don smiled, "May I offer my two pence?"

I nodded and he continued, “I won’t take credit for these words, much of it has been said by my old brothers, but it takes many stepping stones to get from a place to a place that is worth being at. No one does it unaided, and what gets you there is also what matters when nothing else does – family,” he paused, “this life of ours, this is a wonderful life. But it’s most unpredictable. There are so many ways that it can take a turn for the worse, and when that happens, what you need is for your blood to stand firm beside you.”

“Fine words, but clarification then, those stepping-stones that you mentioned, are those people? What sacrifices must we make for blood and does distance and time turn blood to water?”

The Mafioso smiled. “No sacrifice made is too big. The bonds of blood run deep and far, and time is immaterial.”

“Is a sacrifice for life bigger than a sacrifice for money? Who can measure it and how?”

A thoughtful expression appeared on the Don’s face. He nodded at the dealer who stepped forward, “I’m sorry to interrupt, but we digress here a bit. Are we ready to play?”

The Don nodded.

“No,” I said, and walked out of the casino.

5
Caesar

Paris
August, 2015

I have little idea of what came over me. There was anger here, along with a measure of desperation.

"Where to, sir?" I had walked into a taxi.

"Can you take me to Paris?"

The taxi driver looked back over the front seat, "Paris?" he seemed unsurprisingly unsure, "the one in France?"

"The very same."

Perhaps the request was more outrageous than he was used to, for he seemed a tad perturbed.

"Sir?" he finally asked again.

"Paris, I want to go to Paris, the one in France as you so eloquently mentioned."

"I'm not allowed to take you out of Switzerland in this taxi."

"Why?"

"I don't know. That's the rule, isn't it?" he said.

"Rules, shmules, what's the worst that can happen?"

"I could lose my license."

"You don't need to worry about that."

"Sir?"

I pulled out a wad of cash out of my coat pocket and dropped it on the seat next to him.

"How about you drive while I explain?"

I had to plan this carefully.

"Do you know where you want to go in Paris?" he asked.

We had been driving for a while, and if my geographical orientation wasn't too far off, we would be near the Swiss-French border by now.

"I'm not sure, I'll tell you when we get there."

The sun was beginning to break free and dispel the darkness when we finally crossed into the confines of the city. I could see the driver's probing eyes in the rear-view mirror now that we were closer to the destination.

At some point of time during the drive, he had carefully stowed the money into the inside pocket of his jacket.

"Drive around for a bit, I would like to go towards the far north-west of the city. I want you to slow down near any unusual graffiti."

We were driving alongside the golden waters of the Seine, the gleaming hulk of the tower stood dominantly in front of us. I liked the Tour Eiffel better in the early morning light when it looked imposing yet vulnerable, the steel grey resolutely standing ground against the changing hues of the sky.

The 19th arrondissement was one of the poorer parts of the city. A different form of society functioned here, as if all the nays of the world converged in the centre together, here in this little quarter. Before long, the street hawkers would cover the space on the sidewalks, selling everything from oranges to cheap handmade jewellery. A whole rainbow would erupt, a rainbow of skin colour and a rainbow of lives lived.

"Stop."

The driver dutifully slowed the car.

"This isn't one of Boy's works."

"What was that?" the driver asked.

I had spoken out loud.

"I don't want to alarm you, but at this point, the less you know, the better it is likely to be for you."

The fear and concern on the driver's face amplified.

Boy hasn't come up in our story so far, has he? What a folly!

Where do I even start? He is important. He was a man that solved problems, and through some rather unfortunate events in our shared past, he had come to owe me one. Actually, our opinions might differ on that last part, for I suspect that he might feel that he had paid me back in full already. We would have to find out.

"I should be getting back to Zurich. We have reached Paris as you requested, perhaps you could take a local taxi now." His hand moved protectively over his chest in a frail attempt to indicate that he had earned the right to keep the money.

"In a little bit. I need you to make this one last stop."

We drove like that till I found what I was looking for. The eyes stood out, then the unmistakable thrust of the chin, the hair pulled rebelliously against the direction of flow. You could not make out any discernible features, and yet I was sure it was her.

I did not need to see the scribbled initials at the bottom of the street art to know it was Boy's work. The letters 1UP were scribbled at the top right of the graffiti. A little space under it was the number that I was looking for.

"May I borrow your phone?"

The driver's hesitation was palpable.

"This is the last favour I ask you for today. I'll let you drop me off after this."

He slowly passed his phone back to me and I tried to suppress the haste that I felt while keying in the number. How long had it been since we had last spoken?

Boy answered on the first ring despite the hour; the man never slept.

"Who is it?" There was a reassuring familiarity in the gruff voice. He had helped me find my way back from the abyss at one point of time in my life; granted he had also been the person to put me there.

"It's Caesar," I said into the mouthpiece. "I have a problem; can you help me get out of it?"

The click as the line disconnected was my answer.

Interlude

I
Octavia

Somewhere unknown
August, 2015

Questions. Answers. In the end it's all just words. My name is Octavia; you may have heard of my plight. Some men knocked on my door the other day and told me that I had to go with them because my brother was in trouble. I had given up on him years ago and yet the fact that he would come back to haunt me was hardly surprising.

I've been stuck in this cold dark room for over a week now, two maybe. I stopped counting the day I realised I was a dead woman.

Michel de Montaigne once said that if you grow up lifting a calf every day of your life, then years later when you are an adult, and the calf has transformed into a full-grown bull – you'd still be able to lift it. He meant it metaphorically, comparing bulls to customs. My bull is my suffering and I have begun to carry it with pride, for what alternative do I have!

For the past week, I've carried the suffering of captivity like a calf on my shoulders. Now that I've gotten used to its weight, I can carry it on my shoulders with aplomb. I've never been a fiercely happy person, but neither have I spent the best years of my life buried in the mellow sedate desolation that I saw enveloping some people around me. My existence has moved between the shallows of routines and mounds of randomness. Now that I am stuck in this room, I've begun to understand the spectrum of my existence more keenly.

They did not do anything to me for a few days. I began to worry that I'd lose the contentment I found in that stinging familiarity. I found a nail in the corner of the room; it took me three hours to pry it free. When I broke the plaster around it slowly with my fingers and had it loose, I wedged it under one of my fingernails. I then spent the whole day slowly pushing at the nail and tearing the skin underneath bit by bit. Slowly building up the pain and then letting it subside. I repeated the process over and over, creating new troughs and discovering new plateaus.

The next time they hurt me, it won't be so bad. The next time they gave me a shot of vodka with food, I would understand bliss again.

If I scream too much, they give me painkillers. I stop screaming but I never take the pill, I've ripped the mattress in the corner, and I've been saving them inside it. I have seven by now. How many do I need for this ordeal to end? Why did I never search for that information when I had the chance? Nobody ever searches for this kind of information. I was always struck down by the depressive morbidity of the act.

He wasn't a bad boy, my brother. He was just consumed by the selfish arrogance that often accompanies youth. Back in 2005, he was the cool brooding kind and all of my friends thought that he was good looking. Well, he may not be able to get me out of here, but I have seven friends who are waiting for their chance to help me escape.

I didn't realise that in all my musings I've given away all my secrets to you, but something tells me that I can trust *you*.

II
Victoria

Motril, Spain
August, 2011
Tuesday

We believed in love – Amir, August, and I – but we did have our own ways of loving.

But wait – let me start at the beginning. Amir was my boyfriend in those days. All his friends called him 'Boy', a vestige of the life he had once left behind, but I never liked that name. Some years ago, he had managed to acquire a small run-down shack near the edges of Motril and had patched it up to make it habitable. The first floor had three rooms. Amir and I used one, the second was a guest room, and the third had been empty until the day Amir brought August along. We had a couch in the living room that nobody ever sat in – that privilege was reserved for the front porch from where we could see the sea in the distance. It was a quaint little place. We'd have lazy brunches, walk around the tiny city, read, sit out in the long evenings watching the sun dive past, drinking, eating, thinking, and following up with the Descartian train of thought – *being*.

August usually started his day early with a swim. He was the only one of us who used the massive gift of the coast of the Alboran Sea. With the sun shining over his wide shoulder blades that cut sharp silhouettes against the blue of the water, he'd walk in. There was a kindness in his golden eyes punctuated by a happy, infectious abandon. He spent his days volunteering as an English teacher and afternoons reading poetry on the porch, all of this was when he wasn't away on some abstruse trip or another. He played poker to make money. Never too much so as to dream of a better life, just enough to exist. He was gorgeous.

Amir was another matter. There were two discernible sides to him. The loner would spend his afternoons locked up in his space, working on one thing or another, painting, drawing, sketching his own warped version of the world. At some point when he'd get tired, he'd bring his art into his words and transition into a philosopher steering the conversation around him and filling in the gaps where the thoughts of us regular humans feared venturing into. He was good looking, his wide forehead notwithstanding. I want to describe how he looked, but it is hard to isolate the man from the mind. He was gorgeous too.

What about me? I knew an astute observer like you wouldn't miss that.

I was happy.

It wasn't just the lifestyle; there was peace, and there was excitement. Caught between two men who loved me, I could observe how people express that passion in completely different ways. Amir quoted, where August listened. When the artist withdrew, the companion surfaced. Amir was exciting and yet unfulfilling, while August was the perfect foil, he stepped up. I'd be sitting on the porch when he'd come and sit beside me and make it all easy.

We'd sit like that, quietly clinging to each other's bodies for hours, till Amir would materialise and August would gently pass me back to him. The evenings belonged to Amir – long kisses, urgent sex. They traded me like a crystal doll between each other, one passionate man to another. One protecting me, one hurting me, but both loving me.

Did I love both of them? I've thought about it. Would it be a lie to say that finding an answer to this question scared me, no? For the answer might have represented a choice. I loved Amir more than August, that much I can say. But sometimes when I sit and wonder, I must question if that would have been different had I met August first.

I find it fortunate that I met them in that order, for if I had understood love with August before Amir, I wonder if he'd have been as willing to cede control. I did love August, just not as much at the time.

But then what happened, you ask?

August left one day. Just as he'd come, he vanished. One morning, all his things were gone. All that he left behind was a note saying that he'd be in touch. He took a part of me with him. Why is it that the true magnitude of love is only understood with its loss? Why is it that happiness when left to itself shrivels and turns into something morbid, obese, searching and yearning for newer thrills, till you lose what you have?

***

Thursday

I have understood the ironical gain in loss. *Happiness*, or love, is fickle, and it makes you live under the constant threat of desertion lest you provide it with more. More what? I have some thoughts, but I haven't been able to narrow them down to a word, or few words, yet.

An interesting thing happens when you lose something. It makes you less in a way, but if perchance you manage to reclaim what you lost, reclaim only what you lost, then the mere '*sense of more*' satisfies the beast that happiness is. It willingly curls up among its false chains next to your feet, fed for another moment, satisfied for another day.

***

Friday
More energy? But if energy is life, does it boil down to the fact that happiness can only exist if it is provided with a healthy dose of life? What happens when you are completely consumed and have no life to offer? I was never good with these questions.

III
August

Motril, Spain
August, 2010

We sat inside for a change. Boy's agent was visiting, and we had set up the dining room table for the occasion.

His agent was trying to make a case for Amir to come to Paris, "I keep saying to you, Amir, your hermit painter image worked for a while, but if you'd like to sell more paintings you need to do a show. I can set it up easily."

"No," was all Boy said.

"But then," the agent sputtered, "I find it hard to understand how you even manage to live off the few paintings I sell for you."

Amir and I exchanged a dark look at that statement before I turned my head away.

"I'm going for a short swim," I said softly to Victoria.

"Don't go too far," Vic called from behind as I stepped out onto the patio.

I turned to nod at her, but she had turned her attention towards Boy. Her arms lightly wound around his waist, her head resting against his arm.

I threw my shoes off and dashed onto the wet sand.

I sought the *burn*. I ran straight into the water and began swimming towards the island. It was farther than it looked. I wouldn't get back for dinner. Victoria would be displeased, but then the morning shall come, and all will be forgotten. It took only a while before the burn entered my body, sweeping through my biceps and chest, before settling around my shoulders for a while. My thighs heaved and I stopped to paddle in the water for a minute to see how far I'd come. There was still a chance to turn back and make it back for dinner, but what could be gained out of it tonight? I dove forward into the darkness, the grey silhouette of the island stood out in front of me.

The burn kept me going, I broke water and pushed forward again, climbing the waves, and sinking back into them. A familiar wave of comfort took over me as the heart battled to supply the body with the oxygen it needed to keep living. The burn brought forward a surge of dopamine that took away any feeling of despair. I'd found that out by accident, but once I had *it*, I never let it go.

Boy hadn't been surprised; he never was. "A balanced mind can only come forth from a balanced body." One might wonder how he knew that, since he refused to put his body through even a second of physical effort, unless you counted all the sex. A twinge of jealousy erupted within me, and I pushed harder, screaming out at the heat coursing through my body, which retaliated and swallowed me whole.

Sometimes Boy would take a pill when he was down. "I can't think when my body isn't responding, when it is trying to focus on other problems such as why my endorphin levels are low, it refuses to function. When my body is slow and my mind preoccupied, I produce bad art. If all of it is left unfettered, I go on a downward spiral. It is essential to arrest this flow and set it right. Taking a pill helps me get all those rebellious hormones in order until I finally draw something good and become naturally happy."

But I didn't need any of his pills because I had the burn.

I lay on the sand alone on the island. I absorbed the raging calmness of the silence, the stars glistened in the distance, their balanced energy resonating with mine.

Why had I done what I'd done?

It had been the most rational choice at the time.

Why can't I keep this rationality with me at all times?

The mind does not work like that. It is used to focusing on the trivial, the short term, even the irrational sometimes. I need to tame it. The first step was clear, the burn. What came next?

Late into the night when I sneaked back into the house, I rummaged through Boy's bookcase. Nietzsche, Schopenhauer, Spinoza, men of great lore reigned over here. There had to be an answer in them, somewhere.

I heard a rustle behind me. That was Victoria. Her arms slid around my waist, and I hungrily pushed myself backwards into her embrace.

"Food is on the table," she kissed the back of my neck.

I couldn't suppress a sigh of contentment from escaping me, "I'll eat," I said. "I just need to find something to read first."

IV
Maurya & all of his unfortunate friends

India
1970-1992

Truly, the 1970s was the most miserable of decades. There were a lot of futile deaths, and the bombs rang loud over both the east and the west, but you know of all that already. I know little about regional politics and even lesser about war. The cricket team, in the meantime, managed to scrape through two forgettable world cups.

The 70s was like a rebellious teen who had finally realised that the threats of physical abuse that most Indian parents fed their children in the growing years would never truly be realised, and she spent every day in a reckless abandon pushing the boundaries to see what craziness she could reach before they tried to reign her in again. But they never reigned her in, and the craziness escalated to a point where it became the norm.

It wasn't all hopeless, some good things happened at that time as well. Like a hopeful sunrise after days of dark storms, a new country to the east was born. Towards the end of the decade, the greatest of all Indian all-rounders debuted for the cricket team. But before any of these hopeful, semi-miserable or completely miserable events had come to pass, on what must have been a cold night in the heart of winter, Maurya was born.

His father choosing to name him after the greatest dynasty in the history of India might have given a hint of his intentions for his child's future had people been paying attention.

Father was an epitome of discipline and authority. Every morning Maurya had to pass a careful inspection under the eyes of his progenitor to make sure his school uniform was in order. Every evening he would be escorted to cricket practice where he showed some promise, but not enough to please his father. A tutor would be waiting for Maurya at home three evenings a week post the practice and he would guide our young hero through the most complicated mathematics puzzles in his life. Dinner was followed by an hour or so of reading of a carefully selected book before bedtime.

So distressed was Maurya by his father's constant attention that he prayed night and day for another sibling to arrive and share the burden. His prayers were finally answered in the eleventh year of his life when one fine afternoon, news was brought to him that he'd be presented with a young brother or sister soon.

The winter that year brought both light and darkness for the family. Young Maya prematurely entered the world a month before everyone was expecting her. No one was more surprised than their unfortunate mother, who did not survive the torturous labor and traded her life for her daughter's.

Maurya's father took this misfortune as stoically as he did every other setback in his life and refocused all his attention on his young children. The daughter, still too young to have a sport prescribed for her, was assigned to the gentle care of a nanny. Maurya was subjected to twice the amount of cricket training as Father tried to redeem a semi-bright spot in his life. The only positive to come out of it for poor Maurya was that mathematics tuitions were relegated to two sessions a week.

Life moved on, as it so often does, both within the household and outside of it. When the mid-eighties set in, people realised that they might have been judging the 70s too harshly.

However, one event must be recounted in some detail because it would prove to be highly relevant to the children's fortunes. Father's work in the construction industry took him far and wide across the country in those years. He had astutely timed his entry into building nuclear plants right around the time that everyone was beginning to clamour for them. As a result, the family fortunes wealth-wise had developed rapidly. One fine morning in May of '87 he took a short flight to Madras, followed by a quick helicopter ride seventy kilometres south to Malakkapam. He arrived at the plant a few minutes past 2 p.m. to attend what was meant to be a routine meeting with the general manager about delays on the construction of a new reactor. The site had run into minor supply problems and had fallen a little behind schedule. While usually this issue fell below the pay scale of both the men in the meeting room, recent political events in the country had required some attention-grabbing buck passing. The formal reprimand was to take about sixty minutes, and if it had gone to plan, Father would have been in and out of the city in two hours.

As it happened, the general manager was surprised by a visit from the Minister of Energy himself who, perhaps, doubted the efficacy of the exchange in deriving the desired results and wanted to get a word or two of his own in. So it happened that a small issue was soon transformed into a bigger issue worthy of being solved by influential people, and Father decided to miss his return flight at 5 p.m. in order to personally resolve the cause of the bottleneck and get the construction back on track. The next flight was at 10 p.m., which meant that he had a few hours to put the fear of god into his top managers at the plant and then drive up to Madras for the plane ride home. Maurya was going to open the batting for Punjab's under 18 team early next morning and Father wanted to be fresh and ready to see his son in action.

As it turned out, one of the managers had left for home early that evening to attend his daughter's birthday party. The unfortunate father had to be summoned back just as his little girl was about to blow the candles out on her cake. In his hurry, he would forget the keys to his office which housed all the important purchase orders, and he would have to beg pardon of his very displeased boss and cycle back home. By the time the problematic purchase orders were identified and the supplier contacted, it had already clocked nine in the evening.

Father, at this point, knew that catching the night flight was no longer an option. The anger at missing his son's game hardened his resolve to find a solution to the problem there and then. It was a good thing that he stayed back because the supplier in question didn't take very kindly to being disturbed that late in the evening, and a call had to be made to his supervisor's supervisor in order to generate the required sense of urgency.

Finally, it was about midnight before the manager on the other end promised that the orders had been identified and organised and would be dispatched the first thing in the morning when the kind folks in charge of the logistics would arrive.

The group on the site finally relaxed, and one of the men in the office chose the moment to bring out a bottle of whiskey for a celebratory drink to mark the end of a needlessly arduous day. It was perhaps Father's resignation at not being able to make the game combined by a little guilt at having run his men hard that day that made him stay for one night-cap before getting into the car for the drive to the state capital. One drink had just turned into a second when they started hearing the sounds of the alarms coming from Reactor 4.

The man dispatched to check the cause of the alarm came back with the information that a routine test was ongoing on the reactor, and it shouldn't come in the way of one more drink.

It wasn't much later that an explosion went off two kilometres away as the crow flies spewing radioactive material over a ten kilometre radius and destroying a fair few buildings in its path.

***

Father got sick quite rapidly and stayed sick for a long time. The exposure to the radiation slowly set in and consumed his vital organs. Once he knew that he wouldn't live for too long after the fateful event, he meticulously set about putting a plan for the future of his two children in motion. Maya was sent away to live with some relatives for a couple of years, after which she'd be sent to a boarding school. Maurya would stay on in the city under the supervision of his tutors. The business was sold off to a friendly competitor and the money entrusted to Father's trusted manager Vishnu Gupta who invested it into a trust fund to be made available to the children when they turned of age.

Maya had the worst deal of them all, one might argue. She wanted to stay on in the city with her brother and her dying father. However, Father wanted to spare her the pain of seeing him die in the formative years of her life. He took solace in the fact that at least he'd leave her a rich orphan. Maurya hadn't realised how much he loved his sister until she was about to be sent away, and in a moment of rebellion, he tried to assume the role of the patriarch and forbade her departure. But the years where he would command, and people would listen, were a long time away. The strict Vishnu Gupta intervened and ensured Maya's departure.

Maurya dutifully kept playing cricket as his father slowly withered in front of his eyes. Father finally ended his acquaintance with pain a few weeks after Maurya had turned eighteen. He played out the cricket season out of respect and finally hung his pads just as a new summer began.

***

One would not have faulted Maurya for thinking that he had hit rock bottom in his life at the tender age of nineteen, but the truth was that misfortune had just begun its gentle tryst with him and would stay close for a few years more.

Vishnu was a harsh master, harsher even than Father had been. But loss had hardened the young boy in many ways. Vishnu Gupta was displeased when Maurya decided to pass up on an opportunity to study business to focus, instead, on learning more about the construction industry. Maurya felt that the immediate future was in building something simpler – roads.

"It is a difficult industry to break into." Vishnu warned Maurya. Road construction contracts at the time were given out by the government as tenders to be bid on and the industry itself was run by a cartel.

"Five players build all the roads in India; they have divided the country into territories that they guard with all their guile and guns," Vishnu told Maurya. "Even if these tenders are open bids, only one bid reaches the development authority at a time. The process is rigged, and the cartel has their hooks in at all levels." Vishnu was referring to the few thousand government workers in the development authorities that relied on cartel bonuses to supplement their income.

"That would mean that they could put in exorbitant bids and the government would have to approve them since there are no competitive proposals?" Maurya asked.

"That's a part of it," Vishnu answered, "but these substantial margins beyond the cost of goods needs to be split between hundreds of '3rd party interests' in the government offices. These cartels also run small private armies to protect their interests and keep their workers in line."

"Can we figure out a way to work with the cartel?"

"Why would they let you in?" Vishnu asked.

"That's what we need to find out."

Audiences with the cartel were hard to come by, and it took Vishnu the better part of a few months to set up their first meeting. The regional interests in the North for the cartel were managed by Dhanraj Nanda.

He was in his mid-forties from the looks of it and had the bearing of a man who had lived all his life in the luxury of knowing that he would always lead a luxurious life. As far as personalities go, he was extremely unremarkable: the hair had been diligently dyed to remove all traces of grey, while the plumpness of his cheek and a couple of bulges around the stomach indicated that he favoured his food and alcohol, and avoided exertions of the physical nature.

"You should go back to building power plants," he said, "leave this government business to us old folks."

"That business is gone, Mr Nanda," Vishnu said. "We'd really appreciate if you'd let us do a project or two here, just to make ends meet."

Dhanraj pointed an admonishing finger in Vishnu's direction, "I've seen a million upstarts like you who want to come into my business. Let me tell you this for the first and last time. I'll let you sleep with my wife before I'll let you take my business from me. The cartel does not let others play. I give you an inch today and you'll seek a few feet tomorrow. Before I know it, you'll be going for the village."

He mistook the emerging apathy on Maurya's face for dejection and his expression softened a bit, "Young man, I respected your father most days of the week. Heavens know that I never liked him, but he seemed to be a guy who would like a straight conversation so I'd give you the same – if you try to build a road in my area, you will not survive to drive on it.'"

"Is that a threat?" Maurya asked quietly.

"It's a warning." Dhanraj got up to indicate that the meeting was over.

"You can come work for me if you like," he half joked as they left. "I could use a diligent site manager."

Maurya politely declined the offer.

After a few weeks of deliberation, he and Vishnu decided to power through and test Dhanraj a little.

"How many people does he have in his little army?" Maurya asked.

"I'm not sure, around fifty maybe," Vishnu said.

"Well, we need some bullies of our own."

"And how would we pay for them?"

"Let's break the trust fund."

Vishnu disapproved of the idea to start paying off protection money at a time when they didn't have any incoming cash from the projects, but Maurya had taken some of Dhanraj's condescension to heart.

"Get rid of the anger, Maurya," Vishnu had said, "we won't win this if we are driven by our egos."

The rational solution was to hire one notorious thug with very little to lose and fifty of the old workers that had worked for Maurya's father at some point.

"Without any workers in the company, we cannot bid for projects," Vishnu said, leaving out the part that without the projects, they had no way to pay the workers.

"This is *Boy*," Vishnu introduced their hired gun to Maurya, "he'll stay close to you from this day on."

"Good, what's his name?" Maurya looked at the man who looked on quietly on the proceedings disinterestedly.

"*Boy*, that's the name. That's what everyone calls him at least." Vishnu said, "Some stories go that even he doesn't know his own name."

That particular piece of information seemed to be trivial enough for everyone involved to move on without any further enquiries.

Moving on, projects were still hard to come by. They found out upon investigation, that even though their applications were submitted in full, one document or another kept getting lost on the way to the approval board through clerical errors.

Vishnu started the slow process of finding and tracing these clerical errors and carefully resolving them with donations and gifts to make sure the application reached their final destination. All of this happened while the idle workforce slowly ate into Maurya's savings. It would take another six months before Maurya's company won its first tender.

But the news must have reached Dhanraj because Vishnu and Maurya were greeted by a chopped goat's head being thrown over the gate that night.

Before the first bag of concrete could be mixed, half of his employees were intimidated into leaving their jobs by Dhanraj's little army. Maurya countered by increasing the salaries of the ones that remained – an idea that Vishnu wasn't entirely pleased with.

"It is not just these workers that you'll pay now," he said. "What will you do when you need to hire more people and they demand the same money?"

"We'll find a way to pay them above the market rate if we keep a little less money for ourselves," Maurya reasoned.

The duo knew that this wouldn't be enough, so they set about strengthening their political support, "We only need an MLA or two on the fringes of the state."

"Dhanraj's men have put one of our guys in the hospital and the rest won't go to work," Vishnu updated Maurya one afternoon.

"Well then Boy can potentially put a couple in the hospital as well."

"Hurting Dhanraj's men will only turn this into an all-out war," Vishnu had said. "One we can't win with one soldier."

"Not Dhanraj's men, ours," Maurya said. "They need to fear us more than they fear them."

Boy restored some order as per Maurya's intentions, but by the time the first project rolled forward, the workers' morale had hit an all-time low. They finally captured support of a local MLA who agreed to back the new guys in exchange for a sizable donation to his re-election campaign fund. Maurya and Vishnu incurred a sizable loss because of all the unforeseen payments into the Indian approval system, but the duo had finally cracked the correct operating model.

"You don't learn about all this in business school," Maurya joked.

The second project they got had a much higher price tag for the government because Maurya had to factor in the payments to the many clerks and the occasional MLA, plus a token to the local police. Dhanraj's threats continued ceaselessly, but Maurya and Vishnu kept taking the hits and powering through. Boy did his bit in keeping the workers in line and as more funds became available, Vishnu invested in extending his own army and they became more adept in fending off Dhanraj's attacks. They usually bid for obscure projects in the outer regions of the north that Dhanraj did not bother to go for, and slowly a semblance of peace was restored.

Vishnu used the opportunity to rapidly rebuild their political and administrative network. He had become adept at oiling the administrative wheels around them and soon the documents stopped vanishing from their bids. Life moved on rapidly, and by the time the tenth year had passed since Father's death – Maurya was beginning to make a name for himself in the road construction business.

He had also managed to free some of the workers in his small region from the brutal employment of the cartel and they, in turn, were pleasantly surprised to discover concepts such as employee rights.

"Let's build cheap housing for them. If they have a place to live – they are less likely to leave." Vishnu advised Maurya, who took his mentor's guidance and went above and beyond by also building a school and a hospital to go with it.

When Maurya finally paused for breath, he remembered his little sister and word was sent out that she would discontinue her studies at the boarding school and return home to her rightful place.

"Why is this important?" Vishnu asked.

"It is my duty to take care of my sister."

Ten years ago, his frail father and Vishnu had intervened to send Maya away. This time around, nobody could argue with Maurya, and just like she had left, Maya came back on a Sunday afternoon.

Over the years, Boy would become both Maurya's bodyguard and his enforcer. Whenever worker behaviour or tensions with Dhanraj Nanda's troops threatened to derail work, he would be sent out to restore order. It usually meant breaking a bone or two, and on occasion a person would be killed. In a country of a billion people, it was none too big a sacrifice to be made for the sake of progress.

Book II

6
Caesar

Amsterdam
July, 2006

"This is such a colossal disaster," I muttered through the beer froth.

"Surely it's not as bad as you think?" Sumer's voice rang out on the phone.

"My wallet's gone, so has my phone and passport, and along with it, everything else I came with. I'm pretty sure that my eye is on its way to turning a brilliant shade of purple. Till a half-hour ago, I had loose change in my pocket that added up to a little over four euros. I've just spent that on this godforsaken non-alcoholic beer!"

"You can drink to good decisions," his unconvincing attempt at gentle irony failed to appease the young gambler.

"Dude, are you even listening? I was mugged, robbed and feel more than just a little bit violated."

"Are you happy with your beer?" Sumer asked.

"What do you think?"

"I sense discontent."

"That is a mild understatement – but after the day I've had, I'm going to let it slide."

"Aren't I fortunate!"

"Stop messing around. Come and pick me up." Paris was five hours by road, four if I was driving.

"Are you kidding me, you are a million miles away, and I have a date with this very cute Puerto Rican girl I met at Deux Magots last night. Can't you just take a taxi?"

"I've tried but nobody wanted to drive a million miles."

"Whose phone are you using to call me?"

"A girl at a bar."

"She cute?" I turned around to look. She wore a simple brown skirt and a black top. Straight hair, brown eyes, she wasn't wildly pretty, but nothing seemed to be off from where I was looking.

"I suppose."

"Does she have a real beer?"

"I think so."

"Then hold tight for a bit and hang out with her tonight. I'll be down tomorrow afternoon to get your sorry ass back home."

"What the... *France*, Sumer! I'm penniless."

"It's not the worst you've been in. I'm sure you'll figure out a way. All the best luck to you, little traveller. I'll see you at the end of the voyage, or tomorrow, whatever is closest."

I resisted the urge to slam the counter, and after a few calming breaths refused to restore a feeling of peace, I resorted to my age-old nihilism. "Nothing truly bad can happen, when nothing really matters," I said to nobody in particular and turned back to the not un-pretty girl.

"I take it that the call did not go very well?" she asked me as I gave her the phone back.

"Not spectacularly well, no."

"Is there anything I can do to help?" She had a nice pout now that I looked more closely.

"That depends – do you know of a place where I could play poker around here? And would you be willing to lend me fifty euros in return for an adventure?"

I gave her my most reassuring smile. Something must have worked, because she nodded.

When we walked out of the casino ninety minutes later, she was draped across my arm like a starving boa constrictor, "How did you do that?" she asked.

"What do you mean? You were right there."

"I was… but I've never seen anyone play like that. You were like a man possessed."

"I'm not sure of what you saw. I lost more hands than I won," I said. "I lost big and won a little bigger."

"That was quite an adventure, thanks." She leaned up to land a quick peck on my lips.

"That," I began, "barely qualified as an event. The real adventure will begin now." I slowly slid an arm around her waist and gently pulled her closer till I could feel the soft curves of her breasts nudging me softly in my chest. "We need to figure out a way to repay your kindness."

"How do you propose to do that?"

I pretended to think for a moment, "How about we rent a yacht and fuck our way to Croatia and back?"

7
Caesar

Southern Spain
July, 2006

I like the sun, it brought the feeling of a gentle fire slowly burning your body, sometimes threatening, often punishing, but always tantalising, never following through with the purported destruction.

The phone rang and I pulled my eyes away from the brunette who lay on the deck chair next to me. How long had it been? I had left Amsterdam with Joyce three months ago. We hadn't made it to Croatia after all. For some reason, the joy of spending three months on a small boat had worn out quickly for her. I couldn't, for the life of me, see anything wrong with spending the day lying in the sun with an interesting book and an ever-present glass of Rosado by the side.

But after about a fortnight, Joyce said she had to get back to work. We dropped her off near Bordeaux. If you insist on confining your life within inconspicuous barriers like work, there wasn't much I could do about it.

"What's up?" I said into the phone.

"Are you ever coming back?" August's familiar calm voice came over the other end.

"I'm not sure. Do you think they'll let me graduate if I don't?"

"I'm beginning to doubt it. You can't play or pay your way out of every jam.

Carina turned over. She was tiny, but the curves were plentiful. We had met in San Sebastian and then slowly made our way down south on road. She was cute and satisfied with doing surprisingly little in a day. Right now, the sun reflected on her bronzed body. She had taken off her bikini top so as to avoid those *hideous* tan lines, as she liked to call them. I personally didn't mind the tan lines, but I wasn't going to object to her walking around topless.

"Well, I'm almost out of money anyway, what does a man do when that happens?"

"Well ideally, he doesn't run down his bank account in the first place, but if it inadvertently happens, then he comes home."

"Fine words," I said into the phone. "Did you call me just to share these precious pieces of life advice?"

"Well," he said, "there is a game in Paradise City. It's 25,000 bucks to get on the table, it's made for us. If we win, then you wouldn't need to graduate, and I can quit school and open my Search fund."

Carina finally got up in all her lusciousness, ran a hand through her hair lazily and gave me a wide smile. She was a fine girl, but hard to support financially. "I think I can do that, but I don't think my new girlfriend would be thrilled. She is quite used to the... lifestyle."

"Well, come down for the game and then get back to her, and maybe we can get you to take one of those exam thingies while you are here."

"I'm on my way. See you soon," I said into the phone and disconnected.

Later that evening, Carina and I had a brief and uninhibited conversation, the details of which are not entirely important. We made no promises of meeting again, kissed goodbye and parted ways. And I was on my way back to the fairest town of them all.

The place I called home. Paris.

8
Caesar

Paris
July, 2006

August, Sumer, and I lived like kings. Why wouldn't we? Wasn't that the sole purpose of existence? Pleasure was the greatest good mortals like us could hope to achieve.

We maintained a substantial apartment in the middle of the city. The Tour Eiffel gleamed victoriously in the distance. We probably had the most expensive housekeeper on the continent. She cooked like a dream, kept the house clean, and ensured that the liquor cabinet was always full.

One might wonder, why I chose to live outside the town as much as I did when I could enjoy such luxury here. I'd come to rationalise it as this – the fact that I could afford such luxuries and then chose to squander it gave me a certain amount of pleasure. The pleasure that comes from the power of possessing something. Like buying a bottle of Dom Perignon and then pouring it out. I never did that, pouring down good champagne was stupid, but that's not the same as saying it never happened in the house.

The boys threw me a welcome back party.

"Fill your belly, day and night make merry, let the days be full of joy. These things alone are the concerns of the humankind." Sumer was educating a pretty sophomore, "and here you have the pleasure of making the acquaintance of Jules, *the Caesar* himself," he announced me to the small crowd around him, "back from his latest conquest."

I said hello and moved on.

Where was I? Yes, we had simple rules, we played to live. The money came and went, and whoever could pay the bills for the month, did so. I imagine it is easy to do that if you are a bunch of successful players on the fringes of the world of illegal poker.

The others managed to attend a class every now and then. They had an eye on other careers after this party was over. That is where we differed; I was a lifer. Play, party, die. Some insightful people I had met along the way had told me that this might change after a while. I did not doubt it. To be honest, I almost sought it. But wherever I looked, I didn't like what I saw, and *this* worked, so why bother with change?

"Where have you been this time?" A tall blonde handed me a glass of wine. There was a smile on her face, but the stiffness in her bearing lay somewhere between distrust and hostility.

"Around, I've been … recuperating."

"Recuperating from what?" she asked me.

"You know, the vagaries of life."

Her laugh was practised, my mind was usually numb to these trifling demands for small talk. Sumer liked to manage the crowd. I liked to stay at the edge. I chased conversations, and of late fewer and fewer people had managed to keep me engaged. So, I chose to spend my time with myself, along with the occasional girlfriend of course. Does it make me sound egotistic, chauvinistic, or sexist? I'm probably guilty, but I'd beg you to refrain from judgments for a while more.

"Do you have the same philosophy as your friend?" my new companion asked me.

"What do you mean?"

"Pleasure above everything else?"

"Why do you want to know?"

"Just like that, I've wondered, how you could live with yourself, you know, with being a complete degenerate and all?"

Straight for the jugular, we probably needed to curate the invites to these shindigs a little more. Sumer had a thousand friends in the city and all of them and their friends were welcome at our place, provided they dressed provocatively. "What's your name?"

"Zara."

"What is the cause of your questioning, Zara? Is it to learn something, for perhaps I can justify to you about how we live and what it does for us? Or are you, instead, trying to confirm some pre-formed bias that you'd like to pin on us?"

"Does it matter?"

"It does."

"Why?"

"So that I can give you the answer you deserve."

"Wouldn't you rather give me the answer you believe?"

"If your aim is to judge, then I'd satisfy your query just so I can walk away from this conversation quickly."

I digressed for I barely had an answer for her. There were elements here and there that I understood, and yet the more I reflected, the more I realised that there were things that were beyond me.

She looked away for a minute, "What if I tell you that the purpose of my enquiry is personal, that I have a personal curiosity in your life?"

"Then I'll tell you this. I live right now to gain as much joy as I can, while moving towards a goal. My goal is to understand, that's what Spinoza said, right? I'm not a Spinozist, no. I do have a desire to understand things. The first step of my enquiry is the self. I slowly add elements to it from the outside. I'm compelled to believe that experience is an important part of living, and joy is a good baseline to start with. Changing things little by little, so as to be able to maintain that level of self-fulfilment while absorbing more of the world. That is why I do what I do and live how I live."

Her blue eyes had a twinkle in them now. "Is there a limit to joy, and what happens when the lack of *more joy* itself becomes a source of empty disappointment?"

A laugh escaped me, "Do you really expect me to have an answer to *the pleasure paradox* when generations of hedonists have tried and failed?"

"You don't really know anything, do you then?" The twinkle in her eye died an instant death.

"I know very little," I admitted.

"Just as I thought," she said and turned to walk away.

I couldn't help but curse myself. I had given her the answer that she didn't deserve.

A tap on the shoulder alerted me to August's presence, "Welcome back, Prince."

"Couldn't you have arrived a few minutes earlier and saved me?"

"Oh, I was here all along. I thought I'd enjoy the contest for a bit. She cornered me last weekend! For some reason, Sumer keeps inviting her." He leaned in and put a familiar arm around my shoulders, "Now that's done, let's get out of the noise."

9
Caesar

Paris
July, 2006

"Come now," Sumer said, "We need to get to this place."

"Why?"

"Because that is where the fun is tonight."

"What if I don't want to be somewhere fun tonight?"

We haven't spoken much about Sumer at all. He was a rollercoaster, one that kept going higher and higher and refused to go down easily. His downers were as dramatic as his peaks, long and hard.

Sumer laughed, "Why would you want to not have fun?"

"That is not what I said."

"That is what you meant."

He was persuasive and while I'd hate to admit it to anyone else but you, I had a fear of missing out. Epicurus said that to find happiness in a moment, all you had to find was calmness and balance it with an absence of pain. When there was a hot party to get to, the concept seemed almost abstract.

"Juli, let's go."

So we ended up at a villa on the outskirts of Paris two hours later. It took only a few minutes for Sumer to vanish into a crowd near the pool while I lounged around the bar. It was the house of a popular local football player. I caught a glimpse of him as I navigated through the crowd. All of nineteen, soaked in fame and champagne.

Sumer was beginning to scare us. Of late he wanted bigger and bigger thrills. He chased them, and we chased him. Who was I to judge? Up until three seconds back I had been running at the same speed, and it wasn't so long ago that I had registered the pleasure paradox. I was beginning to get so caught up in running that I was now running past the things that used to gratify me well enough not too long ago.

The more pleasure became a goal, the harder it had become to achieve. Every morning we woke up soaking in the little lakes of joy that we had created the night before, and yet by the time the evening arrived those very joys seemed drab and dull. We needed to find another river to jump into.

I tried to share these floating thoughts with the bartender, "The answer is in front of you," he said.

"What?"

"No, literally, drink, man. Stay in the moment. Don't think too much. Take a sip, swirl it around, feel the flavour," he had a near ecstatic expression on his face, "Swallow it. Do you feel it burn its way down?" He looked triumphant, "Any time you find yourself asking stupid questions like the purpose of existence – drink!"

I toasted to his great wisdom and bottomed out my glass, "Great words all, but can we repeat this with gin instead? Good whiskey is just wasted on me."

The big game was coming up. We were playing for a pot of one million euros. It was a lot of money for three college dropouts, or well one drop-out and two slow graduates, to blow up. Sometimes I regretted our close-to-the-edge lifestyle, spending everything we won which now put us on a race against time to make the 25,000 euros we needed to enter the game.

I walked around for a while more, enjoying the moment of tranquility that I had managed to buy myself. The party had shifted inside the villa.

Sumer sat at a table playing poker with the owner of the house. I could see that he had been milking the soccer star for a while now.

"I'll raise," Sumer said, as his opponent reached to match the bet.

The *turn* came next, after which Sumer raised his bet again. His own cards remained untouched in front of him.

The curly haired teenager he was playing was beginning to get visibly flustered as he reached into his chips to keep up.

I watched the expressions on their faces as my friend raised his bet yet again. "Are you even going to look at your cards?"

"I don't care about the cards," Sumer smiled.

The man went all in and lost.

Sumer joined me a minute later, stuffing his new-found money into his pockets. "You missed the fun. I was hoping we could play him together and take a bit of the new contract he signed this week." He turned around to wave at his now former opponent. "But as it turns out, I didn't need your help after all."

Sumer saw me looking at the sullen loser of the game. "Don't worry about him, for someone to win, someone has to lose. Paris are playing Strasbourg next weekend, he'll put a few balls in the net and be all good to go again. What about you? Are you ready to go?" The last bit was directed at the girl who had attached herself to his arm.

"I am."

I was the designated driver, partly because it would have been difficult for Sumer to drive while he was having sex with the girl.

"Can't we wait till we get home," the girl asked as she threw a hesitant glance at me while Sumer pulled her blouse off.

"Don't worry about Jules, we are all brothers here. We share everything."

My eyes locked with the girl as Sumer proceeded to line her left breast with some cocaine and snorted it. “Save some for him,” she said with what was probably meant to be kindness.

“Too late,” Sumer said as he pulled her down. “Don’t worry mate. After I’m done, I’ll drive, and you can move to the back seat and play with Cara here.”

I sped up.

“My name is Zara,” I heard her say.

“Whoo, I feel alive!” was what Sumer managed as a response.

I drove faster.

10
Caesar

Paradise City
July, 2006

We went through a series of games one after the other. Twelve days of going in and out of rooms, slowly growing our little pile of nothing into something. We patiently factored our cash accounts and grew them little by little.

The key was to not run yourself ragged by the time the moment of truth arrived. We needed to be fresh and unbiased to be able to make those all-important calls that would define what we managed to take home. The best thing to do was to take turns at the tables. We played, we won or occasionally lost, then came back and handed our holdings to the next person.

It needed a certain amount of trust to manage this, trust in the person's ability to play, and their willingness to not cheat the others. I wonder if it was friendship that kept us going, or was it just a carefully established balance that none of us seemed inclined to break? Nobody had an incentive to cheat as long as we made more money together than we would make alone. This would go on till the day that the pot became big enough to supersede all the pots to come. What would happen when the winnings of one game would be enough to cover everything we'd win over the course of a decade? How much of it would be enough for one of us to be tempted into taking it all away at one go?

We were all brothers, we said occasionally. But we knew this – it wasn't blood that tied us together, it was money. And it would inevitably split us apart.

"We can't avoid the question any longer, only one of us can play in the tournament tomorrow."

"Do you think you are up for it?" Sumer asked.

I nodded, "It's not like I can trust you to take all that cash into the game, can I?" A note of honest irony had crept into my words in the guise of sarcasm.

"I wasn't keeping count, but I'm positive that I multiplied the money the most in these rounds," Sumer said. "I'd be happy to let you play this. That way I can actually spend some time socialising with some of those beauties around the house while you sweat it out."

"Piece of cake." *Piece of cake*. A million to lose. A million to win. A million to steal.

11
August

Paradise City
July, 2006

Jules was one of the last three men on the table. His face was a mask of calmness, his movements were precise but those who knew him well enough would have understood that he was a nervous wreck by this time.

He excused himself from the table and headed towards the washroom. By the rules, the dealer would continue the game while Jules was away, he would automatically play the blinds.

He had breezed through the first half of the day easing into the games trying to not give away too much of his style while observing the players that he played with. The tables were picked at random and shuffled after the game timed-out.

Slowly people had won or lost their way out of the tournament till this last table.

The final eight had been a difficult group. As solid as you'd expect in a play like this, with a different level of calculated aggressiveness than we had come to experience before. Jules had stuck it out, staying slow yet sure. He had taken a couple of big calls, but they had fallen his way.

The dealer halted the game as the second last player finally lost everything he had on the table. The last man left on the table had been immovable as a rock all day. Jules had struggled to read him earlier in the game and lost a large hand.

As if on cue the young gambler returned. His eyes were red.

"What's the name of the guy?" Sumer asked the person standing next to him.

"Maurya," was the answer.

"What's his problem?"

The man next to him laughed, "He is the richest man in Paradise, he doesn't... care."

"I sure as hell hope Jules knows this," Sumer whispered.

The dealer had laid out a pair of threes on the table at the flop.

"Terrible hand," Sumer was at the verge of losing it.

They were almost done, Jules had picked a hand, and he was not going to back out from it.

The dealer rolled over a 7. They exchanged a few escalating bets till Maurya chose to head for the wall, "All in," he said.

"I'll call it," Jules said.

The dealer carefully counted out his chips as the crowd waited with bated breath. The million-euro hand was on.

She flipped Jules' cards, he had an 8 and a 10. Maurya had a pair of Kings.

Sumer could not suppress his groan, "There go the silicones."

The dealer flipped the next card, it was a 9.

"No."

"6 or Jack," Sumer whispered what everyone in the room knew. "He needs a 6 or a jack on *the river* to win this hand."

The dealer flipped the last card over, and the face of a bearded king looked back at the room.

"A pair and three of a kind win," she said as Sumer went down on his knees.

12
Caesar

Paradise City
July, 2006

Never play a man who has nothing to lose.

I had borrowed Sumer's stripper money to stay on in the city for a few more days, "Come home with some of it. We still need to make rent." Those were his last words to me before leaving.

How do you rise above something like this? We hadn't come in with a lot of money of our own. But we were going to leave with a lot less than we had hoped to leave with.

A woman approached me with a bottle of champagne. "I did not order that."

"Compliments of the gentleman over there."

I looked at the man standing in the balcony above the floor I was sitting on. Maurya's face smiled down at me. "He requested if you might be kind enough to join him up there after your drink."

What was the point of sending a bottle of champagne to someone if you expected them to walk away from it immediately afterwards? "Certainly," I said as I poured myself a glass. I'd go after I was finished with the bottle.

It was a funny bar, more like weird funny, something out of place funny.

It was an anomaly in the city where glitz and glamour rolled off the streets, straight into the gutters. This place was normal. In fact, it was more normal than most places I'd been in as long as I could remember, including the house we called home. I could never go back there. My life in Paris was done. Perhaps someone else would take over our little castle, perhaps it'd slide into ruin. I looked within myself, but it was hard to get myself to care.

I sipped the champagne gratefully; the cheap beer had been far too expensive. Apparently, the simplicity of the place did not extend to the prices. It was still a place that the inhabitants insisted on treating like heaven on earth.

The floor was crowded with people in their early twenties, well my age. It was funny that I felt that I was older than the crowd. Again, funny as in unnatural, perhaps it had something to do with the fact that I had been calling the shots around me for far too long, making my small world bend to my will so much so that I'd begun to feel that I controlled it. The feeling of age was followed by a feeling of frailty.

"How do you like this place?"

My tormenter had chosen to come over to me.

"It's nice. Simple. No frills."

"Thank you, I'm glad, that's the intention," he said as he settled down next to me, ignoring my uninviting expression. He probably felt that the bottle of champagne had brought him the right to my company.

"Do you own this place?"

He was staring keenly at me. "Yes, in truth, I own all the places on the street, and the next street." He smiled. "I own a lot of places around the town, but forgive me, that was not your question."

I shrugged. If he could have a conversation with himself and walk away, it was fine with me.

"I've heard a lot about you," Maurya said.

"About me?"

"Caesar, Cesaré, the king, the stories of how you went through the ranks playing games around the town to come up with the cash for the tournament are beginning to assume legendary proportions. I think the fact that you lost it all at the end is probably helping the legend grow even more."

"Legends can go fuck themselves if you ask me. I'll happily take the million instead."

"And then what?"

"Then what, take it easy for a bit, and then come back to the table a few months later, maybe years if we could make it last."

He nodded. "I've heard those stories too, how you move from resort to resort with a girlfriend or two." He poured himself a glass from my bottle of champagne. "How are you holding up?" he asked.

"What do you mean?"

"Mentally?"

"Well, I'm beginning to get somewhat tipsy, you know with the champagne and stuff. This line of conversation sure isn't helping the mood. But apart from that, I feel ok, sort of."

He smiled, "I was asking about holding up after losing the game."

I didn't answer. It hurt.

"I used to play cricket when I was growing up. I was almost good at one point. I thought at the time that with more practice, inspiration and mentoring, I could break into the big leagues."

A man came close and leaned forward to whisper something in Maurya's ear. He was dressed like a page 3 elite but had the bearing of a bodyguard. Maurya's guards probably made the page 3 in these parts, especially if he owned the papers. He nodded and waved him away before turning back towards me, "Where was I?"

"You were telling me about how you were about to crash the cricket party on the block."

He smiled again. It was a calm reassuring smile and for a moment the hard-faced man I'd played against was gone. "Of course, well, every time I fell down, my coach would come up to tell me to get up and get moving. Every time I felt I was too tired to continue, he came up and told me to keep working at the game anyway, and every time we were close to defeat," he paused, probably for effect, perhaps because he enjoyed telling the story, "He told us to continue fighting for the win anyway."

He got up, "You've been moving around for a while, you haven't noticed the pitfalls of it because you have been winning all the time. It takes a little amount of courage and some organisation to fight back from where you are. A process if you like. I need to go and meet some friends, but I may have a job for you if you are interested. You'll make back the money you lost in no time *and* have a chance to go back stronger. The question is: do you have the strength to get on with it?"

He tossed a card on the table. "Come up to the room in forty-five minutes if you are interested and we can talk more about it." He smiled the warm smile again, and as I watched, it melted away into a cold hard stare, "And if your answer is anything but yes, I want you to get out of my city before the night is over."

13
Caesar

Paradise City
July, 2006

What did you think I would do? I was out of work, close to homeless and almost certainly penniless. I was sinking. The lifeboat that showed up to rescue me turned out to be a yacht. So what if it was the devil incarnate's yacht? Nobody really likes their boss. I was stopped at the door of the suite by a man who looked like a proper bodyguard. There was no page 3 duplicity about him. He carried a gun in plain sight.

"Let him in," Maurya's voice came from behind.

"We are almost done," he said to me before turning back to the men in front of him. The box on the table was lined with crisp notes. They looked warm to touch. Well, that's how all money looked to me, so perhaps the analogy isn't perfect.

Maurya nodded at a guy who picked up the bag and replaced it with another one. One of the men tentatively looked up at me before opening it. Maurya followed his glance, "You can trust him," he said. No, you can't, my head objected.

I hope that you'd pardon me this slight digression, but I must share a theory that I have come up with. Do you think I lost the money because I considered stealing it? My subconscious told me to lose everything so as not to be presented with the difficulty of a moral decision? The more I think of it the more I'm certain that it couldn't have been that.

My moral compass had been fairly flexible all my life, and it was unlikely to change just at the moment when I needed it to not fail me. Well, there goes, it was just a theory.

Back in the room, another suitcase was duly opened. I don't mind delving into the occasional party drug to take events to another level. I don't share Sumer's proclivities towards complicated narcotics, but I didn't need first-hand experience to be able to see that the box was full of neatly lined bags of cocaine.

Maurya hadn't taken his eyes off me the whole time. At that moment, I understood what this meeting really was. It wasn't a meeting between friends, or even a deal. It was a test. He wanted to see if I had the stomach. I had no idea how much I'd given away in those few unguarded moments. I'd know soon enough; a man like him probably didn't spend much time dabbling around with idle chatter.

The men were swiftly shown out once the transaction was completed. Maurya stood up to walk to an alcohol cabinet towards the corner of the room. "Would you like a drink?" He didn't wait for an answer.

He motioned towards the balcony and handed me a glass as we stepped out.

"My need for you is simple," he wasn't a man of many words apparently. "I have many hotels and casinos around the town. We like to maintain a pleasant retreat for people to come down and play. People come for the gambling, and they spend money on alcohol, beds, escorts, and other luxuries. It is a simple and profitable part of my business and I'd like to keep it that way."

He paused to light a cigarette, "Of late, we've had an outbreak. Gamers like you, looking to prey on the leisure players are coming to the town and scaring my tourists away. These people do not care about sustaining the flow, they care about making the bucks and running away to the next town.

They are slowly destroying the revenue sources by scaring my patrons away, hurting us in the process."

He took a sip of his whisky, and then concluded, "I won't have that."

His voice had become cold which contrasted classically with the warm night.

"What do you want me to do?" I asked. "I can tell my boys to stay away, but..." My boys, were they still my boys?

He gave me another one of his appraising looks, "I want you to play for our side."

I took a sip of the golden fluid floating in my glass.

"You'll play with the house money, so you'll have endless resources, seemingly. But the one thing you have to be able to do is to not lose. *Ever*. I want you to not just beat these guys. I want you to draw blood, drain them, destroy them to the extent that they never play again."

I laughed, "You seem to have an inflated estimation of my skills. I'm a player, not a psychoanalyst. I can do math, I understand how cards work, I also understand how people think, to a lesser extent, but I cannot manipulate them the way that you seem to think I can."

He looked out of the window over the city, and I followed his gaze. We were on the forty-sixth floor of a building and a thousand gleaming diamonds twinkled back at us from the street below, "You are better than you think. I've seen it, but you lack direction. People like these," he paused, "people like you, and your friends, there is one thing that you love and that is glamour. You may not even understand it, and yet you crave it. You win it, violate it, and almost never appreciate any of it," he paused.

"The people here want to win, but one thing that they want more than that is to win from the best, and by presenting you to them, I'm giving them the big game. Only they'll play with a mirage; all you need is a little humility and then you'll be unbeatable, but they wouldn't know that because they'll think of you as they think of themselves. *Avaricious, incorrigible and insatiable."*

He laughed as he continued, "You are a rational man, aren't you? The life you've been living, Jules, you may not know it yet, but the answer is this – you've peaked, too early maybe. Your friends have begun to feel it too. The only way from here is down."

"Three things can happen. One, you continue trying to do what you were doing, fail endlessly, till the time you lose all capacity to try. From then on, you'll live a shadow of the life you had and then spend evenings regaling people with stale tales of how life used to be when you could keep Miss Puerto Rico drunk for the whole summer. That is probably what is going to happen to your friend Sumer."

"Two, you change the way you live. You take the best of what you have, your mind, leave out the parts that have been destroying you, and make something out of it. That is the path I want you to take."

He moved his hands as he spoke. If we hadn't been speaking about how to keep his gambling and drug haven running, the conversation could have well been mistaken for an older brother gently berating the younger.

"What's the third?"

"What?"

"The third alternative, of what happens to people like me?"

"I thought I wouldn't need to tell you that after the first two. Well, something drastic happens, something that fools you into believing that all the time that passed hasn't really, that you don't really feel the fatigue that you feel. It makes you go on for a few more years, and it might even seem you are doing better than ever for a while, but this is like running headlong towards a cliff edge. One day you will reach it and keel over."

He grew silent after that. His body relaxed, and he put on the cold drug lord face again which inadvertently sent a shiver down my spine.

"I'll make a simple deal out of this for you. Stay here with me for a year and I'll give you half a million euros. If you do what you do well, there are other things that you can do for me once your assignment is over. If not, you can walk away with the money, no questions asked, and continue living your degenerate life as you please."

What he wanted me to do sounded like a boring job. If you take away the thrill of winning and the risk of losing, Poker became purposeless. Yet, Sumer and August were probably halfway across towards their investment banking careers. This seemed like a fairly measured, tailor-made exit for me.

"I'll take it."

He held out his hand. The brotherly smile was back on his face. It was hard to imagine that I was talking to the same person. "Welcome to the team," he said genially.

Interlude

I
August

Motril, Spain
August, 2010

"What would your ideal world look like?" I asked Vic. Her slightly wet sun-kissed brown hair flitted across her slender neck before sweeping downwards over her tanned torso. A tiny birthmark stood out gently in the middle of her chest, escaping the careful camouflage of her blue and white bikini top. We were sitting on a table at the porch. Amir was in his attic leaving the two of us to our afternoon musings.

"An ideal world around me, or an ideal world that could ever exist?"

"Either," I said. I had spent the last seven months trying to find a blemish or an imperfection on her face, anything that made her look less gorgeous, a hint of ugliness that I could cling to, but I had no success so far.

"*This* is pretty ideal."

I had to struggle to keep looking at her face as she leaned forward on the table to grab the half-cut avocado. "You, Amir, I. I don't want much else."

We spoke of inconsequential things for a while.

She moved closer, one of her hands curling around my upper arm, hugging it close as she rested her head on my shoulder.

My elbow nudged her soft breast. I kept looking resolutely at the paper in front of me. My mind had resorted to abstract scribbles in a bid to recapture control over its thoughts.

"You know, I worry about this sometimes," she finally said.

"What?" I asked.

"Losing you."

I finally seceded and turned my head in her direction; she looked up at me.

"Losing you, losing Amir, losing this peace."

I pulled at the arm that she was holding to and reached down to hold her hand, our fingers entwined effortlessly. I cupped her cheek with my other hand, lifting her face ever so slightly higher, tracing my thumb lazily across her cheek. We both sat like that for a while. Our eyes now locked into each other's, now gazing at the other's lips.

"Peace is a state of mind," I said as I chose to drop a peck on her nose instead, "It comes and goes."

"You know what my ideal world will be like?" she said. "It'll be constant, like a lost island that never changed because it was never touched."

I kissed her nose again, this time on the tip, ever closer to her lips. The look in her eyes questioned me as to why I didn't move any further.

"But what of time? It'll touch you and change you."

She looked troubled, "What if I refused to change?"

"I don't think it works that way." She freed her hand to pluck out a tiny leaf that had blown into my hair, then pulled me slowly downward to deposit one of my kisses back on my nose.

"How does it work?"

My thumb was now caressing her ear, the fingers gently massaging the back of her neck, "We change, even when we don't want to. Every thought adds itself up to everything you've thought of before, and, passage of time changes the perspective a bit and brings about a feeling of distance to the old memories. Under the influence of all these forces, your perception of peace is vulnerable."

"But what if I fought against these forces? Spent my time keeping all memories fresh and limited all exposure to new experiences?"

"Memories distort with every retelling, no matter how diligent."

"Are you talking about yourself now?"

I laughed, "Mostly yes, but I'm also talking about you."

"I have a plan; do you want know what it is?"

"Yes."

"I'm going to manage this change keenly and slowly, change the bare minimum that I have to. I will look at the most routine, banal, and innocuous parts of my days and I'll change them. I will fool life into thinking it is moving along while I stay stagnant. Unmoving. Unflinching. How is that for a plan?"

The lips parted as she flipped her tongue across them. I turned my head at a movement. Boy stood behind the closed glass patio door looking out at us. He watched us for a few more seconds, then turned around and went back inside to his studio.

"This is an ambitious plan. Can you promise to call me and tell me how it goes?"

She laughed, "I won't have to dummy, because you'll be right here, watching it happen."

***

It was a summer afternoon like any other. Vic, Boy and I, were at the beach and through no fault of our own, a neighbour from the house next door had invited himself into our company.

"The Mrs is out in the town," he said as he plopped himself down besides us. His sun-greyed hair and a leathery cast to his skin indicated that he had seen a few years in his life, though it was hard to say how old he was.

I'd spent the last few weeks being led amok by one book or the other, from Spinoza to Schopenhauer – who would have known that it was to be an unassuming neighbour who would unravel the riddle? *What would it take to survive this life?*

It was a steady, slow progression of topics, from the sun to life in Motril, to life in general.

"I never think about what I do," the gentleman finally said.

"That must lead to some fairly questionable decision-making?" Vic laughed.

"*Au contriare*," he smiled. "I feel like my decisions are less disruptive or destructive and aligned towards a positive life."

He waited for us to ask him to elaborate and continued by himself when nobody did.

"We humans have a habit of obsessing on the why. Every time we have a decision to make, we iterate over alternatives. We stress over them and go back and forth over the implications of a decision before arriving at something. That is because our boundaries as living beings are caught between who we implicitly are and who we explicitly think we are. *But you know what happens in the end?* There is a convergence and coherence between eventual decisions. At the end of all that thinking, we wind up doing the same things that we were likely to have done without spending any time in the agonising assessment process. Maybe not always, and perhaps not exactly the same thing, for another thing happens after we finally make a decision – we assess. We *agonise* over it long after it has stopped being relevant, and at the end, we modify our behaviour ever so slightly. The whole process is inefficient, and if that wasn't bad enough, we try to extract learnings and modify our behaviour from one experience at a time, which in all honesty, does not stick."

He paused for breath and waited to see if anyone would venture a question and continued when nobody did.

"The answer to the conundrum is what philosophers of old have called the virtue ethics. A guidebook for human behaviour if you please. There are, of course, many guidebooks, for there are many schools of thoughts you could subscribe to. All you need to do is try to find if one fits with you more closely than others. Once you know where your ideologies lie, the next steps are simple. First, every time you arrive at a decision point, think about what the school prescribes – love, laugh, fuck, fall back on the action and execute it. Just like that – bam, done, inefficiencies eliminated."

"Next, find a moment of solitude after some time has passed. Long enough that you can squeeze together some experiences, and short enough that you remember what happened. In that moment of solitude, reflect on things. Remember what you did and how it affected you and those around you. Reflect on what sort of gratification it brought you, and did that gratification persevere beyond the moment? Reflect on whether that decision made you more or if it made you less. The act of doing it all together, like a monthly review, helps you to be objective in your assessment. When you apply a level of rationality to the decision, you are more likely to change for the better, or for what you think is better at the time. Fun. Boom. Evolution. Change is that simple. see how I've cracked it. In a few simple steps, you can reduce the burden of living."

He sipped his beer. We just assumed that he would continue and had settled into a quiet thoughtful stupor that comes from a combination of wine, sea and not caring.

Boy finally spoke up. "I thought the burden of living was the most important bit."

I pondered over this interchange till late in the evening. I did not know it then, but Boy had already dropped a key that would help me open door number 3.

II
Maurya and all of his unfortunate friends

India
1992 –1996

A quick word or two must be said about Vishnu Gupta. He was a stoic consequentialist. As far as was possible, he strove to live by virtue and honesty, and yet when the matter came to do something bad for the greater good, he never hesitated.

This would come to pass when local competition reared its head and the threats resurfaced. After ten long years, Maya was back in the city. She was now fifteen. Maurya and Vishnu's company had slowly managed to take a small chunk of contracts from the cartel. The cartel had been tolerating their presence. Over the years, Vishnu had built both political relationships and their private army. All these efforts were staging measures for their next set of expansion, which included acquiring their first state-wide road project.

By now, the cartel had seen enough. It decided it was about time that their little enterprise was finally shut down. Maurya understood both true anger and fear for the first time when a car in which Maya was coming from school met with an 'accident' that ended up killing the driver.

"I'm going to kill Dhanraj Nanda," he had said.

"Maybe you will, maybe you won't. But that won't get you the victory that you seek," Vishnu had interjected.

"What will?"

Fortunately for them, Vishnu had a plan, and a sound one at that.

Dhanraj Nanda's family had run the cartel's business in the North for the last thirty years. Vishnu and Maurya had been summoned into his farmhouse for a chat. In the few years since they had met the last time, he had acquired a significant paunch and a young new bride.

"I admire your perseverance," he said, "but I cannot allow you to do any further business in my area," he said. "I've turned a blind eye on your activities, but like I had feared, I gave you a finger and now you want my hand," he wagged the aforementioned finger disapprovingly, "it is not going to happen."

"There has to be a way for us to co-exist, Mr Nanda." Vishnu said, "If anything, that is what we've proven over these past few years. You do not have the capacity to do all the projects that pop up in the north. A lot of development projects have been delayed by five-ten years. If we find a way to co-exist, you won't lose any business and we'll be able to execute the projects that you cannot do."

Dhanraj had shaken his head at that, "What's in it for me?" He continued without waiting for an answer, "I only see a downside; this will create unnecessary friction for the cartel. My workers already believe that there is another company to work for and I've been asked to improve working conditions. What the fuck is paid leave? Why should I pay people for taking time off work?

"Your financial clout and political influence have increased already while mine remains the same. I may not be the most astute businessman, but I know that allowing you to continue in my market will only increase these risks risk for me."

"But it is not *your* market," Maurya interjected, "all of this development is a part of a bigger scheme by the government, the roads are meant to increase regional accessibility and make it easier for other businesses and industries to develop in those areas. By not allowing us to be a part of the solution, you are now creating a problem that will condemn large swathes of the country into prolonged ruralhood."

At some point during the discourse Dhanraj's wife had come in through the door, "Amita is a lawyer," he introduced her with some pride. "Cornelia Sorabji tapped on the glass ceiling almost a hundred years ago when she became the first female lawyer in our country, and yet so many years later law is still a 'gentleman's club'. Amita here is challenging the stereotype. Would you like to sit with us for a bit?" He directed the last at his young wife, "Young Maurya here has some interesting thoughts on the state of the Indian economy."

Amita smiled and dutifully sat down next to her husband. From the looks of it, Dhanraj had at least twenty years on his wife. She directed a kind look towards Maurya in response to her husband's remark. "Don't mind Dhanraj," she said, "his cynicism of the world is increasing at the same rate as the grey in his hair."

Dhanraj smirked in response, "I live in a realistic world. But I do have an answer to your question Maurya. The country will move at its own pace. You are optimistic, and it is not uncommon at your age, but if you run too fast ahead – you will find that you are the only one up ahead. All your work will eventually fall to ruin."

"What did you think?" Vishnu asked Maurya when they were back in the confines of their car.

"Most cynics think of themselves to be realists, but when it comes to this industry, he is probably right. There is only room for one player in the north."

"You are not suggesting that we pack up our bags and leave?"

"No, we need to find a way to win the north," Maurya said.

"Dhanraj himself doesn't care much," Vishnu said. "We need to destabilise the cartel a bit and shake the foundations. Not so much as to warrant an all-out retaliation, but just enough that by the time the dust settles – we have a position."

Vishnu and Maurya started off by setting up shell companies to bid on projects. As new bids started pouring in from all directions, the cartel couldn't find any people to terrorise at these headless firms. The cartel managed to push most of these bids out, one way or another, but as the supply of the people who wanted to bribe them increased, the approvers in development authorities saw an opportunity to demand higher bonuses.

While the cartel struggled to deal with this first problem, Vishnu put in motion the country's first professionalised smear campaign. Suggestive hints were dropped in the hands of revolutionary journalists on some occasions. Carefully purchased news articles started appearing in national dailies calling out corruption around major construction projects into question. Vishnu continued feeding fuel to the fire until it turned into a frenzy that brought almost all of the national infrastructure construction industry to a standstill.

Dhanraj's crushers were shut down under an investigation. The cartel's friends in the government kept finding reasons to stop the investigations and resume the projects, but more and more evidence kept emerging at the most inopportune of moments.

Vishnu finally gave the cartel a visible enemy to aim at by declaring their intent to bid on five major projects in the north.

"What do we do if they start hurting the workers again?" Maurya asked.

"Don't give the workers an option to rebel. We've treated them well and they've been loyal when it was convenient for them. Now it is time to extract the value of that loyalty. Show them that while they run some risk from the outside, dissent towards you would result in certain misery."

Boy was given a new mandate to implement – worker payments were to be paid at the end of completion of projects which could take anywhere between three-six months. Absenteeism was answered by termination and evacuation from housing, expulsion from schools and restricted access to the hospital.

It was around this time that Dhanraj Nanda requested another meeting with them.

"I have spoken to the cartel and they have agreed to let you in," he said grudgingly, "but everything that you've been doing must stop."

"We would stop, but what's in it for us?" Maurya asked.

"Do not get too cocky, boy. You may have won the first hand, but the cartel is still strong."

"You are misunderstanding our intent here, Mr Nanda," Vishnu interjected. "We are happy to cooperate, but I'm just keen to understand what cooperation might look like for us?"

"You'll share the north with me. We'll run our own mini cartel if you please. You'll get a chance to bid on thirty percent of the projects around the region while I get the rest."

"We've won a hundred percent of the projects over the past year," Maurya reminded him.

"It won't stay that way. Give me some time and one of you will be dead and the other may not win any projects next year."

"There is no reason to get testy, Dhanraj," Vishnu slipping into first names did not go unnoticed by anyone in the room, but such was the transition of power between the participants that Dhanraj did not retort and listened on.

"The answer is simple though, we need to split the projects in the north between us, equally, fifty-fifty. I think we have proven that not cooperating is probably more harmful to you than cooperating. And the death threats are getting a little old, you understand that there we have access to guns too."

"You bastards do not have the gumption," the man had not aged well this last year. A fact made even starker by the presence of the angelic thirty-year-old wife by his side.

"Perhaps you are right, but are you willing to find out?"

Maurya and Vishnu left Dhanraj's farmhouse with a deal that had seemed impossible a few years ago.

"We aren't going to let him have his fifty percent, are we?" Maurya asked.

"Not a chance. But now that we are on the inside, the cartel doesn't care how we settle the north. We give him a few pieces here and there until we can slowly ease him into retirement."

"Sound idea." Maurya had a thoughtful expression on his face, "but that might mean that he doesn't suffer enough. He did cross a line with the attack on Maya."

"Don't worry, retirement in this business does not come with a pension plan."

Book III

14
Caesar

Paris
August, 2015

Caesar sat next to the Seine, reflecting on his options. The taxi had taken off. Heading back to Zurich was hardly an option, and running without Boy's help was bound to be a pointless enterprise. The only other alternative was to get a decent breakfast while waiting for fate to have its way with him. He dialled Boy's number again out of the vague hope that something different might happen on a second try.

"I suppose you thought that I'd be dead by now. Good news, I'm not."

Silence greeted him at the other end. *Silence*, we don't use it well enough. It is known to fill comforting gaps in conversations and is also known to convey love at times. But one thing it is more proficient at than everything else is screaming, for yes, sometimes silence screams. Loud.

"I heard what you did in Milano." Boy's gruff voice came on at the other end.

"They have Octavia." Caesar had stepped out of the car with the phone to spare the driver from the details of the conversation.

"That would explain why you are still alive."

"I need help right now," Caesar said.

"You are calling the wrong person; this is on you." The sound of his voice was calm, cold steel, and the words were delivered on the edge of a knife.

"I'm calling the only person that I could call."

"Tell me, Caesar, do you believe in god?" Boy sounded resentful.

"Should I believe in a god?" Caesar answered.

Caesar heard the screeching wheels of the car behind as the driver finally gave up on him and drove off, sacrificing his mobile phone.

"It helps occasionally, like now for instance, for prayer might be your only answer." He disconnected without another word.

Now that he was here, stranded by the side of the river, Caesar realised it might have made sense to think it through before he ran from Zurich. Half a thought also went out to the poor taxi driver. But that was all he could afford at that point. Boy had as much as passed the sentence on him.

He looked at the phone he held and put it in his pocket. It might come in handy. His hasty exit from the casino had not allowed him the opportunity to retrieve his few belongings.

The sun had risen proper over the horizon and now beat down strongly on him.

And so like a man who grew tired of staring and waiting, Caesar turned around and did what anyone else would have done in the same situation. He went to get breakfast.

Mishka caught up with him just as the food arrived. "Fancy finding you here," he said as he sat down at the table. "I should thank you for making me drive all night, but I reserve pleasantries for when we are alone."

Caesar signalled to the waiter who came forward with a plate of pancakes and put them in front of the Russian.

"I took the liberty of ordering you some breakfast," Caesar said as the waiter poured him some coffee.

If it was possible to be truculent in this beautiful gem of a city; Mishka had managed it well. "You speak too much. The games are over, wise boy. I have new instructions. You call the bank right now and ask them to transfer money to the bank account that I give you." Barely suppressed glee lurked under his words now and all of a sudden, he looked slightly less grumpy. "If you do this fast, I let you go with a few broken fingers. If not, then I crush your fingers so that you can never hold a card in your hand again, then I break every other bone in your body one by one, and allow the pain to settle in little by little. I'll also break your legs so that you can't run, then when you start crying for me to kill you, I'll rest for a while and let the bones get better for a few days, and then I'll break them all over again."

Caesar dug deep for the blandest look he had in his small armoury of *looks*, "You paint quite the picture?"

"Don't make jokes, gambler."

"That wasn't a joke, that was sarcasm." He took a large bite of the pancake and a bit of honey dribbled out. "I'm not a huge fan of losing my bones, the way you make it sound it could take a few weeks. I honestly can't stand all that time looking at your ugly face. To keep things simple, I will transfer the money. However, I left all my things at the hotel, I'll need to get back to my room and access my laptop in order to get in touch with my banker."

"I'll give you my phone."

"I don't have his number."

"Can't you google or something?"

"What do you think this is? *BNP Paribas?*" Caesar grimaced. "I need an encrypted device to get in touch with my banker in Cayman."

Mishka leaned closer and grabbed Caesar's thumb in his hand. "You think you are smart, but this time things go as I say." He pushed the thumb back towards the arm till they both heard the snap. Pain swept through Caesar's hand.

"Do you have a counter proposal?" he asked through the pain.

"We drive back to Zurich, go to your room and then you get in touch with your man in Cayman and transfer back the money."

Caesar looked at him in disbelief. "If you really had to break my thumb, then perhaps you could have thrown in an input or two, or if that was too much of a task, then the least you could have done was to rephrase the sentence a teeny tiny weesy easy bit because, *that's the exact fucking thing that I said.*"

"I was making a point," the Russian replied. "Let's go."

"Friggin' brute, don't you want to finish your breakfast?"

Mishka looked between his captive and the plate, and then picked up his knife and fork.

"Do you mind cutting mine into smaller pieces, because thanks to you, I can't hold my fork anymore."

The Russian matched Caesar's look of disdain with his own dose of disbelief, then reached over and pulled Caesar's plate towards himself, "Only fair, I guess."

"Thanks," muttered Caesar, "and after this I'll need to go to the men's room for my morning ablutions. You'll need to help me with some wiping."

Mishka stopped with his fork poised in front of his mouth.

"I'm kidding, you big brute," Caesar said.

"No more jokes," he said. "We move as soon as we finish. More coffee!" he barked the last at the waiter.

"Don't speak with food in your mouth, Mishka."

15
Caesar

Paris
August, 2015

Another day lived. Another day spent getting ever so slightly closer to the silent eternity.

The day streamed past the car. The roads wound down and up, swinging sideways as if dancing in joy to celebrate the beauty of the sun, and Mishka and Caesar hurtled along it onwards towards Zurich. Life would question him someday – someday soon perhaps, but its slow approach would not go unquestioned. Its tentative footsteps would ring true on the creaky front porch presaging the knock, and then the reckoning shall follow.

"What do you think will happen, Mishka?"

"Today Mishka take you to hotel. I break another finger. You transfer money and then I eat ribs," he said. "Not your ribs," he added as a clarifying afterthought.

Caesar smiled at the Russian's single-minded train of thought. "Allow me to rephrase my question." The green fields were interspersed by colourful signboards as Mishka eased the car onto the A6. "When you are done with me, and with everything else that you usually do, what do you think will happen?"

The large Russian peered at him from across the car. "You talk philosophy, gambler? I understand little philosophy. You think a lot. I work. I eat well. I drink vodka, and after everything else, I sleep like lion. I get up. I repeat." He sat back contented, unweighed by the irony. "I also kill little thinking men for boss."

"I am just a game to you, am I not, you big brute?" Caesar said softly. "Tell me, are most people more scared of you than me or less?"

He looked out over the highway and paused before he answered, "I like you thinker, you are funny. I'm nice to you," he said. "I'm less nice to other people."

"I can imagine that, your brutishness." He resisted the will to wag his broken thumb in the Russian's face. They had managed to tie a makeshift bandage around it.

The rushing landscape made it easier for Caesar to forget where he was coming from or where he was going towards. A part of him wished that the journey would go on for a while longer. He found himself drifting off to sleep between thoughts.

A slap on his face brought an end to that. "The fuck if you try to sleep while I'm driving," Mishka glowered. "I had to stay awake all night because of you!"

"And a gentle nudge wasn't good enough to establish that?" The cheek smarted where the Russian had hit him.

"I was making a point."

Mishka's frown had almost receded, which made him look almost jovial. "Good pancakes for breakfast," he said. "Maple syrup and bacon."

His head was turned towards Caesar, which was probably why he didn't see the truck jump out of the exit and ram into the side of the car. The door caved in instantaneously snapping the seatbelt and hurtling the big guy towards the windscreen as the car was pushed off three of its wheels. A wall of glass hit Caesar in the face as the final wheel let go of its hold on the road under the momentum of the turning car.

The front began to cave in as it flipped, once, twice, before finally coming to rest in the middle of the road.

A hand reached in with a crowbar to scrape off the last of the glass on Caesar's window. A familiar face peered down on him. "Are you alright?" Boy asked him as he pulled him out of the wreck, and then half carried him to the truck that was standing about twenty metres behind them.

"Mishka?" Caesar asked.

"Dead," Boy said. "Thankfully." He propped Caesar against the door of the truck. "Here, look into my eyes. I need to see if you are just dazed or if you've knocked your head."

"Knocked my head? I think there was plenty of knocking right there. *What the heck was that?*" Caesar was beginning to come around. "You almost killed me!"

"You asked for help," Boy said. "Do you understand the situation you were in? Not only was this the only opportunity to get you out. This was the safest."

"You killed my Russian."

"Do you think you could have got out without taking him out?" Boy shouted at him. "We need to get out of here right now."

Caesar walked gingerly to the passenger's side of Boy's black Renault and got in. "Surrounded by proper bloodthirsty motherfuckers, which kind of craziness do I have to see next?"

16
Caesar

Unknown village in Eastern France
August, 2015

"Are you ready?"

Boy had spent the last hour patching up Caesar's various wounds.

"Do we have to do this?"

"No other path will get us faster to where we want to be. Over and over again you put yourself in places where you get hurt. I can drag you out of car crashes, but I cannot save you from yourself."

"I have lied and cheated," Caesar finally said.

"Indiscriminately and without repentance."

"What do you want, Boy? I haven't seen you for five years, not in person, stolen messages, email addresses that change after every three months, watching the paintings you leave of her around the world. You want me to pour my heart out to you?"

A look of sadness crept on his face, as if a memory of the days past flitted in front of his eyes. "You've kept it away from your heart for too long." He broke out of the reverie and became his stoic self again.

"The memory has festered inside your head, it has grown into a being, to the point that it has a life of its own now. There are two of you, and you know it. The simple forgiving human being that you were meant to be, the poisonous man that refuses to forgive himself."

"Stop this," Caesar said.

"You'll keep finding ways to hurt yourself, unless you face it."

"I'm a murderer," Caesar finally answered.

The only sounds in the room were the distant dripping of water.

"We often overestimate our role in the scheme of things. Often times, we are responsible for nothing more than just our unfortunate presence when life happens." Boy gestured towards the seat, "But let's talk more about it."

Caesar sighed. "I will, but can we first close the windows?"

"There is no one out there," Boy said but he closed the windows anyway. In the meantime, Caesar revisited the most poisonous day of his life.

17
Boy

Unknown village in Eastern France
August, 2015

"I received a letter for you," I said to him. "It arrived a while ago at Motril, maybe a year ago, maybe more." I handed the thin envelope to him.

"It is from…" Caesar said. "Thank you for holding on to it."

I laughed, "It was the least I could do. I would have tried to forward it to you sooner, but I had nowhere to send it."

He fidgeted on his chair; the memory of the conversation we'd just concluded still had its claws wedged around his heart. I'm afraid that they'll never truly let him break free. In due course of time, all stories shall resolve themselves. But it's his story to tell. We haven't met yet; everyone calls me Boy though a couple of people in this world insist on calling me by the name my mother gave me, Amir.

"How long are you going to keep drawing her?" He jumped from one topic to the other swiftly lest the desolation grab onto his mind again.

"She is my digression," I answered.

"I might need a little more than that to go on."

Over the years, Caesar had come to accept that he could ask me questions if he wished, but my answers were my own, "Do you remember *the question*?"

"*What would it take to survive?*" he answered.

I nodded, "And you know the answer – a digression. For the first few months after she left, I spent all my time trying to understand – why did she leave?" I had to pause at that.

"I drew as I thought, more and more, pictures of her one after another, delving into creases that I hadn't seen when she was here, fighting with the expressions, asking the same question over and over again. Why?

"As I burned through the kiln, I found myself changing and that brought forth another question – *who would I have to be to survive this?*

"I painted her in different colours, the eyes, deep dark crimson now, a piercing azure another time, the nose, the curve of the lips. I changed it over and over; there had to be a hidden message there. So haunted was I by the question, so lost in it, that I didn't realise how far I'd managed to dig deep within the self.

"I digressed deeply, *heroically*. No one can paint her better in the world. Do you know what I found down there? A deep devotion for her. And what did that make me – a votarient? An ardent? An obsessive lover?"

"What are you trying to say?" Caesar had a troubled look.

"The method was the answer. Or well it was a part of the answer, and for that moment, it was enough. I devoted myself to her and found out that I *was a devotee*. That is what I needed to be to survive."

The cloud on Caesar's face cleared up. He took a deep breath as if trying to sum up the perfect words to register his awe at my discovery. "Dude, that makes no fucking sense."

I smiled, "I can understand your scepticism, it would be hard for you to grasp it. It was my journey, after all."

He pondered over it, "And what then?"

"I did not know it then, but the answer occurred to me at a time when I had stopped caring about it. I was enjoying the new-found culmination of my devotion, and it came to me when I painted this." He walked to a covered canvas that stood in the corner of the room.

"I had kept it ready for this day, for I knew it would come."

I tore off the loosely wrapped paper and carried the painting across the room to the little table.

The painting was just lines crossing the canvas in a hundred places, it could be a hundred different things. I could see comprehension in Caesar's eyes, and I understood that a person looking for Victoria in that painting would find her.

"I don't understand," he said it in a way that belied the very words.

"You see, I had been focusing entirely on her all this time, and it was in a moment of cleansing my mental palette I said to myself that *it might be interesting to paint a visage of August.*"

"Before long, implicitly one image progressed into the other as my mind tried to tell me what it had known already – she left because she decided that she loved someone else more than me."

A troubled expression reappeared on Caesar's face. "You know that makes no sense, Boy," he feigned ignorance.

"I'm not saying that any of those actions were deliberate," he said. "If they were, the world would have been a couple of philosophers lighter. But in those days down at Motril, she saw a way of loving that I wasn't capable of providing at the time. At a later time when I had begun to mirror that devotion for her did I realise that, that was how she felt for me. She had been happy sitting at the edge of the room for a long time, looking in at me, never craving for anything more than my presence, never asking for anything that I didn't give her myself, and then everything changed when she finally found out what she deserved. The devotion that I should have given her, that she gave me, that I give now. That knowledge drove her away. While at that point I would have kept her a prisoner of her ignorance, knowing what I know now, it would have been wrong to do so for it freed not just her of me, but it freed me of me as well."

"Now that you've changed, now that you've found that devotion within you, why don't you go and get her back?" Caesar asked.

"If only I knew where to look?" I said. "That is only part of the problem, for all through this she has changed too, for me. My devotion has built her up into an enigma that her true self is unlikely to match, but I wouldn't know it till I see her. I fear to find out, for I might not survive the knowledge of her being any less of a goddess than how I've imagined her to be all these years since she left. Every day these two ends of the ropes tied to my two arms pull at me, threatening to tear me apart."

18
Caesar

Unknown village in Eastern France
August, 2015

"How are you digressing these days?"

"The usual, nothing special. Eat, play, sex. Surprisingly little has changed."

"You have to go back," Boy said to me.

"Wrong answer."

He looked at me, "Not really. If you run, they will kill Octavia, and then you will spend the rest of your life running from them, till they eventually catch you and kill you."

"If you go back and give them the money, and ask them to free the girl, then there is a prayer with your name on it that says they'll let you walk away." He paused. "Though if they didn't have a reason before, they definitely have a reason to kill you now."

"Wait... what? What did I do?"

"You killed one of their men."

"I... you killed him!"

"To get *you* out."

"What good does it do me now if my only choice is to go back?"

"I told you I couldn't help you; I came at your insistence." His face had the infuriating serenity of an imminently violent ocean. "You owe it to Octavia."

"Isn't she dead in any scenario? I've run around for three days trying to think of ways to get us all out of this. Am I the reason she is in there? Or are those brutes who are holding her captive to be blamed? Or is it neither? She is a victim of association, but does that then lay the responsibility of her security on my shoulders? Is one life worth more than a hundred, a thousand?"

"Don't try to fool yourself, none of this money is ever going to help anyone but you."

"Haven't you heard of the term trickle-down economy? Every dollar I spend on a cocktail feeds a bartender somewhere." Caesar uncorked the bottle of whisky on the table and poured himself a stiff drink. "Don't you see, me caring for her is the biggest threat to her at this point."

"You know what happens when you run?" The memory of another chase from years before came back to mind. The culmination had haunted us both for a decade. Could I expect life to be more reasonable now than before?

We sat in silence thereafter. Boy had sprung the memory on me like a bloodied knife that reeked of hatred and betrayal. I couldn't take the fight into the future.

"What are you going to do?" he asked.

"You are not leaving me much of a choice, are you? I have no option but to go all in, again."

19
Caesar

On the road to Zurich
August, 2015

I called Don Camorra's men from Basel. I was pushed to the backseat and handcuffed to the door for my efforts. Being back with the men who had held me to ransom brought back thoughts about Mishka for the first time since the escape. Boy was right in a way. I had condemned Mishka to death when I made that phone call to my mad painter friend.

The weight of the letter in my pocket pulled me down even as the peaceful lull of the green fields threatened to take me away from the reality of my situation. I slipped the letter free from my pocket and pulled out the few sheaves of paper. Sumer's handwriting brought forward memories of easier days.

Mon frère,

I've been trying to reach you over the past hundred years or so, but apparently replying to emails is no longer in fashion.

If I was to guess one of three things has happened, either you are dead, or you've finally gone all Epicurus on this world and run away to become a hermit, or the worst possibility of all, you have been ignoring me. While none of those possibilities fill me with any kind of pleasure, I hope it's not the first. We can't afford to lose another one.

Before I get on further with my rambling, I should tell you that life is going on as well as ever. Still living a few hours off the west coast of Norway, I know you wouldn't believe me when I say it, but the water here is a deeper blue than everywhere else. The Mrs is fine, as is the kid. Back in Paris, I couldn't have imagined ever finding happiness in simplicity such as this, but that is how life changes.

I had an epiphany the other day, or maybe it was an acid flashback, hard to be sure.

Anyway, back to the epiphany, it started off with the memory when I took part in a shamanic ritual in Costa Rica. Do you remember it? I have no memory of whether you were there, maybe it happened after we split paths.

I remember this coinciding with a time where I had been completely swamped with self-doubt that I no longer had any measure of who I was as a person. It was as if a veil had been lifted on my sense of self and I knew that the person I was objectively assessing was far from the person that I truly was. I travelled to this part of the world to be able to close that gap and break my ego and find who I truly was. I think that I had finally realised that my sense of identity had become so poisonous and malignant that no other answer could exist apart from the fact that this wasn't truly me. But who was?

You know what the Buddhists say, that there is no true sense of self, no permanent sense of self in the very least. All that exists is a consciousness and immediate experience, and all else that happens is just our mind projecting our past and future in a frame that is easy for us to comprehend in the present.

We drank some tea made with Ayahuasca. I think the shaman spiced ours up with some roots containing DMT.

Frighteningly little happened in the first hour. I sat on a mattress trying to stay in touch with the vegetative life around me. The peace was punctuated by the occasional sound of someone retching into a bucket.

It took about thirty minutes for the medication to kick in. It was just little flashes of light to begin with. And then little colours started blooming out of the most unlikely places and spouting into little waves before wisping out in a lightless flash. The stars circled around my head as if preparing for a journey to an adjacent galaxy. Don't get me wrong, all of it was fascinating, but no part of this was ground-breaking. Yet.

Then started the life flashes. People say that you sequence through the most important life events chronologically. I don't think this happened. Instead I saw events that seemed to be most crucial to whatever was hurting me in that moment.

First, I saw all those times where I hadn't lived up to the full potential of an event in time. You know all those evenings that we spent together, I found that I had never truly been there with you. Perhaps I had been present in body, but heart and soul I wasn't there, and you know how I know that – because my heart and soul were so scattered that I couldn't have been anywhere.

That is part of the reason that I'm writing this letter, my brother, to apologise for that. I'm sorry, that I skirted through all those years without acknowledging truly what we had. But that part is done, and I'm trying not to make the same mistakes with Raghnild.

But something else happened that evening that is important for me to tell you. It wasn't your fault. I know it now even though I hated you for your part in it then. What else was there to be done? If you fuck over a guy as powerful as Maurya – retribution is hardly a surprising consequence. I saw you both there, which is funny because I hadn't been there in person, but the image was as clear as if I had been sitting next to you on the docks in that little Italian village. I saw Boy's shadow and I saw the look of fear and despair on your face. You were as much a passenger in it as I. I would have made the same choices. As I write the last bit I realise that having the same choices as me can hardly be the source of any comfort. And I don't know if my forgiveness means anything to you, but you have it, should you desire to accept it.

I left the retreat halfway through the programme. I didn't find the right path, but I did see a wrong one. This is the story I wanted to tell you today, and I hope it stays with you for a few days in the very least, if not for the rest of your life.

Dude, send me a note when you've read this just so I know you are breathing. In either case, I hope that you've managed to keep all right.

Till I see you, love,
Sumer

Interlude

I
August

Motril, Spain
August 2011

We had gone on a rare visit into the town. Victoria was uncharacteristically agitated. She had spent the whole afternoon moving around the house, then the evening making some food and in a rare show of anger, she had thrown what she had cooked in the trash.

Boy sat on the kitchen table watching her move around in this state of frenzy. He had tried to appease her earlier in the evening, but she was beyond calming at that point.

We had come out to the town to dance. It was my idea. Victoria was intrigued, and Boy didn't object, so we went.

None of us spoke as we sat in the tiny booth sipping our light beers. She got up after a few minutes of solitary silence and went to sit at the bar.

"Do you want to go after her?" I asked Boy.

"Let her be," he looked at her.

"How have you been?" he asked. He left the real question unvoiced. We seldom spoke about the events that had brought us together, that fateful evening in Italy, when the world had gone mad.

"I'm fine." Both of us knew I was lying, but he left it at that.

The burn helped me and these past few weeks I had spent dabbling in a different form of virtue ethics.

"May I ask you a question?" I asked him.

His expression was bemused but the nod was reassuring.

"That day on the beach you said that the burden of living was the most important bit, what did you mean by that?"

He laughed without mirth, "Of all the people, I would have thought you'd know it best." A measure of unintended scorn had crept into his voice.

"I spoke too soon," he said in a kinder voice. He looked at Victoria who was now talking to a man at the bar.

"Do you know why Victoria was running around the house all day today?"

"I can't be sure."

"The answer is that she was trying to distract herself from whatever was disturbing her. All that running around, cleaning things that didn't need cleaning, cooking things that she didn't want to eat, saying things she didn't want to say, all of it was an act."

The man with Victoria had dragged her out to the dance floor. "What has that got to do with anything?"

"That is what we all do, don't we?" he answered. "We spend all our lives trying to distract ourselves, we live within '*the layer of digression*' as I like to call it. It is the finest human skill, have I ever mentioned that before? Digression, it is the finest human skill. We spend a lifetime living a digression so as not to look at what there is beyond. I apologise, it is hard to not lose myself in abstraction here, but I'm trying to steer away from the rhetoric and tell you the true story. We tend to live our life in this one long digression, moving around understanding the real answer, we chase things laterally when we need to travel longitudinally towards the end. Most people choose to spend their lives in this obscurity. I do it that way, as long as you live your life fairly, without regrets and do not hurt anyone, unless hurting them conflicts with hurting yourself, it is a fine way to do life. Every year I set myself a new goal, a new challenge, or a new desire, sometimes it is to possess things, sometimes it is to experience things, it is all there, and it is fine. But it is also important to remember that while you are overwhelming yourself with digression, you deny yourself the opportunity to grasp the true beauty of living, the burden."

"What is the burden?"

He was looking beyond me. I turned to follow his gaze and saw Vic in an embrace with the man she had been dancing with.

"I don't know what lies ahead. At the end there is absolute death. Final. But there is a layer in between that I haven't managed to break down yet. Some philosophers called it imperishable happiness. Happiness without reason, that is beyond the reach of hormonal stimulants, beyond the reach of self-judgment, beyond digression, happiness that just exists."

He lapsed into silence post that and after about five minutes of watching Vic, he walked away from the table, leaving the keys of the car on the table.

I tried to reflect on what he had said, but the images of Victoria stopped me from parsing them any further. A few minutes after Boy left, Victoria left with the man as well, perhaps to find a dark alleyway somewhere. A feeling emerged within me that hadn't surfaced for quite some time. It resembled disappointment in someone other than myself and I couldn't help but welcome it. This was useful, a new pain could be useful to suppress an old one.

She came back to the table about thirty minutes later. Not a word about what had happened was said.

"Should we head home?" I asked.

"I want to drink some more," she said, and that's what we did.

***

"Did it hurt you when I went off with that man?" she asked me on the drive back to the house.

"Yes."

"Serves you right."

I did not answer.

"We went back to his hotel room."

"Good."

"We had sex."

I did not answer.

"It wasn't very good."

It did not matter, did it?

Somehow it had been easier to see her with Boy. They had known each other before me. They had professed love for each other that preceded me. Yet some part of me had thought that I came next; that if it wasn't Boy, it was me. It turned out that it wasn't the case and the feeling hurt. She had cheated on Boy. No, she had cheated on both of us. Was this just a digression?

"Do you want to know why I did it?"

I did not answer.

"To hurt you."

"Why?"

"For loving me."

I stopped the car.

The only reason I did not scream at her was so as not to give her the satisfaction of knowing that her searing words burnt through my soul. "You hurt me because I love you?"

"I hurt you because I love you."

"That isn't new, then what is?"

"Now, I love only you."

The heaviness of the words hung in the air, but she did not wait for me to respond. She was insistent and earnest as she fought off my hands and kissed me. I tried to push her away out of instinct, but all of a sudden, a year of suppressed desire surged within me.

Her hair smelled familiarly of lemons; her skin was soft under my fingers. It was the insistence of her kiss that was new. I kissed her neck and then bit it till she winced. This would leave a hickey; Amir would see it. There was no going back. I hungrily unbuttoned her blouse, slipping a hand in, the moment I had enough room to break in. I moved my finger over her breast, slowly caressing it, then pulling at it, she echoed my motions with hers. The warmth of her body seeped through me as my lips touched her breasts. She pulled back and lifted my chin so I could look into her eyes. There was a serenity to the moment that is hard to explain now.

The face of the man she had just fucked swam in front of my eyes. I pushed her off me. "No," I said, "not tonight. Not ever."

Neither of us said a word as we drove back. She went straight to bed the moment we got home.

I sat awake for a few hours. Then it was time to throw a few things into my backpack and leave.

II
Maurya and all his unfortunate friends

India
1996 - 1997

Maya came back to a house that was a shadow of the world she had left behind seven years ago. The household she remembered had centred around the strong figure of her father with a group of fawning servants. All that and more seemed to have changed now that her father was gone. The thousand nannies had been replaced by tutors, and the large void seemed to have been occupied by a man that resembled her father in all but half of his name, and yet Maurya could have been a complete stranger to her.

He had rescued her and for that she was grateful, but any emotional connections that she may have felt towards Maurya as a child had been squeezed out of her in the long years away from home.

She brought it up with him over dinner on one occasion, "It is a matter of time," he said, "you were young when you left, and we did not get an opportunity to bond. We'll get to know each other afresh."

Maurya put down a near scientific plan in place to make sure they had opportunities to interact and get to know each other. They would have dinner together most days, and one evening every week was reserved for a movie or eating out – often both. He would keep his weekends free, and they'd squeeze in a hike or a swim. He taught her squash and a game every other evening became a new source of competitive interaction. All in all, he was the most constant and dutiful person in her life. He never missed an appointment, always made sure all her requests were met rapidly and conclusively.

After weeks of small talk, they finally crept into the more intimate discussions.

"Are you sad that father and mother are no longer here?" she asked him.

He paused, "I used to be, but life has taught me that while there is much in the present to worry and be angry about, we also have much to be thankful for."

"But aren't you ever sad that they are *dead*?"

"Sad for us, not them. It is sad for us because we might have missed some time with them, but what would grief bring us anyway?"

"So you never think about it?"

"That's not what I meant. Not thinking about it would mean that I was trying to deceive grief. I acknowledge the grief of their absence, but I refuse to sulk."

In many ways she was in awe of her rescuer.

She had never seen him angry in his life until the day she had an accident on her way back from school. A small truck had rammed into the side of the car. The door on the driver's side had caved in and crushed the man.

She had been dazed and fearful, her mind and body drowning under a wave of hormones that weren't usually there. He had barged past the doctors to her bedside, "Are you alright, Maya?"

"Yes," she said, he looked over the bandages on her arm as if to inspect the veracity of her statement.

For some reason that she couldn't explain, she felt a tinge of happiness at his concern for her. Never had anyone given her that kind of attention. He looked at her as if she meant more to him than life itself. He glanced over at her, his eyes still matted with concern and a gush of warmth rushed to her.

"Oh oh!" The next thought that jumped into her head made Maya realise that all the strife in her life up to that point was going to pale in comparison to the trouble she was going to be in now – because through all of his scientific approach to managing their interactions, Maurya had managed to get Maya to fall in love with him.

Book IV

20
Caesar

Paradise City
July, 2006

I called August and Sumer to tell them that I wasn't coming back.

"What the hell are you talking about?" Sumer asked over the phone.

"I'm staying on here in the city."

"I heard that the first time and it does not make any sense." The anger seemed forced, and I could sense a wistfulness in his tone, as if he still wanted to cling on to life as we knew it for a bit longer. "What the hell are we going to do with the apartment?"

"Move out, maybe stop paying the rent," I said and disconnected. It was fun while it lasted, but it was now over.

Maurya took me around to his most important establishments – the large casino, and the larger casino, and the large casino by the marina with the large hotel next to it. All his friends met me with a simpering smile on their faces and a sceptical smugness in their eyes. They told me at the bar that I did not need to pay for my drinks, and I drank all night just to see if they stuck to their word. They did, and I woke up with a terrible hangover.

"I can't handle any alcohol today," I said to the waiter while ordering brunch by the pool. "Bring me a glass of fresh orange juice and the largest cup of coffee you have."

My eyes turned to follow a tall brunette as she got out of the water and walked towards a sun chair.

"Wait," I said to the waiter as he began to walk away. "How about making that coffee Irish instead? I think I might be able to manage that, and while you are at it, hold back the orange juice and turn it into a mimosa."

He nodded again.

The blue of her bikini matched the blue of the sky. Now if that wasn't a pickup line waiting to happen then I didn't know what was.

"I wouldn't do that if I was you," I heard the waiter say behind me.

I turned around in confusion, "I think I can handle a breakfast cocktail."

"Not that," he had followed my gaze to the girl on the chair who was now drying her hair with a towel. "She is *his* wife."

I didn't need to ask whose wife. The man owned everything in the city. Why wouldn't the most gorgeous woman here be his wife?

Somehow the revelation made me want her more. It is a tough quandary, isn't it?

"I'm ready to have my drinks now," I said to the waiter as he hurried away.

I couldn't help but look in her direction as she lay there. One leg propped up, while the other stretched out, a hand resting lazily on her stomach and the swell of her breasts barely restrained by the bikini top.

Maurya let me spend the first two weeks in abject drunkenness before breaking down my hotel door one evening and threatening to have me thrown out of the city if I didn't turn up at the tables that evening.

I'd have found a way to forgive him if his insolence had stopped at that. But the jerk forbade them from serving me drinks and just like that my castle of dreams turned into a very colourful rehab centre.

I was jittery all day, till I sat down at the table, and suddenly clarity reigned. I was here for a reason, to win. But now that I had the house behind me, it somehow made the whole act seem less thrilling. I hated it. When the poor shmucks showed up at the table and won some money from the poor old fucks who had managed to get away from their wives for the evenings, I'd be shown to the table to even out the odds.

I'd observe them for a while, and then pushed them out of the game, a small hand lost, a large hand won, a little back and forth, till the crippling blow where I took all their money. The reality of what I was doing dawned on me every time I saw them swallow their loss as the dealer turned over the last hand. This was exactly what Maurya had done to me.

I got a message from August and Sumer now and then, and for a while I kept replying. After some time, it stopped making sense to stay in touch, so I had a clerk at the hotel pick me a new phone.

I saw their faces in the faces of the players I destroyed and that filled me with both pity and hatred. They didn't deserve it any more than we had, and yet like the inevitability of a wave crashing down on a sandcastle, they were swept away. I drank myself to oblivion every night after the games.

After about three months of doing this, Maurya began inviting me to his private gatherings. These were usually small events somewhere in a suite in the hotel. Small parties, where the occasional transaction was made, and goods here and there were exchanged.

"I want to introduce you to somebody," he said and pointed at the woman on his arm. "This is Amita."

"Enchanté," I said as I leaned forward for the formal two-cheeked *bizou*. Monsieur Dior wafted off her neck.

"This is Jules," he said, "but everyone calls him Caesar around here."

"Like the conqueror?" she laughed. "What do you conquer?"

I could have said a hundred things, but none of them would have been appropriate in front of her husband.

I shrugged instead.

"Everything," Maurya answered for me. "He takes away a player's will to play. Few possess that skill."

He smiled like a head coach looking down on his prize protégé.

I shrugged again.

I couldn't keep my eyes off her all night. Every time she flipped her hair, I caught a glimpse of her slender neck, a hint of a tattoo sneaked out from under the luscious cascades.

I stopped by her on my way out. "Smiles," I said.

"What?"

The look of confusion dissolved on her face when I said, "*I conquer smiles and make them mine*."

Now that was a stupid thing to say, I thought to myself as I walked out to the waiting car.

21
Caesar

Paradise City
July, 2007

I've always dreamed that at some point when life would do a rollcall and call out my name, I would proudly put my hand up and say, "Present." But then I had lost the last few years in the cacophony of my mistakes. I spent most of those days drunk and as far away from cognizance as I could imagine, and then the days that I did show up, it was after shame had consumed me and spat out a shadow.

It was like any bad relationship, me and my shame that is, if only I had the courage to get up and walk out on it. But no, I was far too dependent on it by now. At some point over the last year, I had slowly fallen farther and farther into the trap. Pleasures of all kinds, and in all proportions were at my disposal. When everything that I desired became equal to everything that I possessed – the will to strive had slowly evaporated.

I woke up on the floor of my room. I looked up at the bed and a couple of girls who worked at the hotel were in there. Some memories of the night before came back. I had brought them up, got them drunk and then fucked them silly, and soon as that was done, I had wanted to get far away from them. The all too familiar shame had begun wrapping its elbows lovingly around my neck, and I did the next best thing – I drank to forget. I remembered drinking some vodka to knock out the final vestiges of consciousness before passing out on the carpet.

I brushed off the cramps and crawled into the jacuzzi. One of the girls joined me after a while. "You really are his favourite."

"Whatever do you mean?"

She smiled. "Nothing, it's like he has many employees, doesn't he? But then all of them are his employees, *you* he treats like a prince."

"As they say, the world reflects back the perception that you have of yourself."

He treated me like a prince. He owned the city and acted like a king. Maybe that was why everyone treated him like one.

I played some poker, beat some kids from the city, and then lay by the pool for a few hours. I saw Amita from time to time. These were my idyllic days.

What did I miss the most? The striving perhaps.

Maurya had kept his promise. I had made my money; it wasn't a crazy amount of money by any means. But it should keep me comfortable for a few years. I understood that the best thing to do now was to leave. But why bother now? In any case, the world wasn't going to change a whole lot in a few weeks. Next month was as good a time as any to leave Paradise City.

One fine afternoon while I was lounging by the pool, Amita got up from her sun chair and walked over to me before lowering herself down to sit near my feet.

"Have you been enjoying your time in the city?" were her first words.

"For the most part."

"Have you been around to see some sights?"

Her black bikini top could do little to contain the life within her as it strained against its restraints to jump out.

"Not that much."

"Well, you should get out a bit, it is such a nice city, ours. I can show you around, if you like."

"I might take you up on that," I said.

She moved to the chair next to me and lay down.

"Tell me, Jules," her voice had a roughness to it. Do not get me wrong, it was a nice voice, but it wasn't the smooth voice of a singer. It carried a real-world edge to it, "How did you end up in our little dreamland?"

What brought me here was money.

"I don't know," I said instead. "I dropped by for a weekend with some friends and stayed because in the word of the great Mario Puzo – Maurya made me an offer I could not refuse."

She laughed, "Well he has a tendency to do that, doesn't he?" There could have been some humour in there. "We are having a little dinner tonight at our place. You should get out of this hotel for once and come." I nodded. The hotel, the club or his house, it didn't really matter where I passed out.

So it was that through an invitation by the queen, after a whole year in the city, I made it into the house of the king.

Maurya had seemed quite delighted to see me. "You've never been to the house? *Really*?"

It was a small gathering.

I was standing by the window when Amita slipped up next to me, "Why do you come to the hotel when you have a pool in the house?" I asked her.

She shrugged. "It gets boring around here."

She seemed to be fairly drunk and put a hand on my arm to steady herself. "You have a nice smile, you know," she said. "But you are miserly with it. What are you thinking about all the time?"

I took a moment to ponder, "Nothing."

She had a patient smile on her face, "Surely, there's more than that?"

"There literally isn't," I replied. "I hadn't even realised that I wasn't smiling. Maybe that's just the expression that my brain defaults to when it shuts down."

Amita looked at me with rapt attention, I couldn't quite understand why.

"I feel it too sometimes," Amita said after a few seconds. "I just get consumed by the *flow* around me and start operating on auto-pilot. It's a natural thing and not something to be worried about. As long as you can recognise the patterns and break the cycle whenever you catch it."

Could I fix it to some extent? Perhaps, every period of rational awareness was usually followed by a wave of overwhelming senselessness. It came and went of its own accord.

We were the last three people at the house a few hours later. Amita had managed to pass out on the couch and slept with her feet on Maurya's lap. For the first time since the conversation on the hotel balcony, I found myself completely alone with him.

"I think you should move out of the hotel."

"Why?"

"The setting isn't right, you have too many people around you all the time and probably never get a peaceful moment. Also, you are stuck in this one setting where nothing around you seems to be stable or real. I have an apartment not far from here. I'll have it ready for you to move in tomorrow."

It was hard to dislike the man when he looked at you as if the primary concern in his life was your safety and comfort.

"All right," I said.

He smiled. My eyes strayed to Amita, her dress had ridden up her thighs. The black fabric mocked me, she moved and lifted her leg slightly. I looked at her for a second too long before pulling my gaze away. Maurya was still smiling at me.

"Can you help me carry Amita up to our bedroom?"

We walked her slowly up the stairs. Maurya held her around the waist while I steadied her on the other side. A slight shift in balance resulted in her falling over me and I put my hand up on her stomach to steady her. Perhaps my fingers lingered for a second or two, her head had fallen on my shoulder, and I could smell her perfume. Maurya straightened her head with a tender caress to her cheek.

I stood back as he slowly lowered her down into the bed.

"You like her, don't you?" he said without turning back.

"What do you mean?"

"I've seen you look at her. I don't blame you; she is an outstanding woman."

I tried to think of an answer, but silence seemed to be the safest haven.

"Would you like to spend the night here?"

"I can just head back to the hotel," I began to say.

"I meant, here, with Amita."

He finally turned around, "You can have her if you like. I can watch."

"But she's asleep."

"Exactly," he said softly, "she wouldn't know."

My eyes went back to the woman on the bed. Maurya reached down to her thigh and slowly slid her skirt upwards, the lace underwear brazenly stood out against the cream of her legs. He curled a finger under the shoulder strap and pulled it to the side until it struggled against the breast, threatening to spill it out.

He raised his eyebrows, as if to question what I was waiting for. I moved forward slowly and stepped by his side. One of his hands went down between her legs and a finger gently slid under the red lace. Amita reacted to her husband's touch by a slight movement of the leg. He pulled his fingers out a few seconds later and placed my hand at the nape of her underwear. Warm wetness engulfed my fingers a second later. Maurya no longer needed to direct my other hand which had found its way up to the zipper at the side of her dress.

Maurya had occupied a seat on a couch in front of the bed, his feet propped up on a small coffee table.

I lowered my lips down to her breasts, before kissing my way up her neck to her ear. I waited for a familiar gasp as I kissed and bit her ears, but none came. All the response I got was shallow breathing.

"She's not awake," I said as the madness crashed down around me. "She's not awake," I said one last time as I walked out of the room.

22
Caesar

Paradise City
July, 2007

I wondered afterwards if Maurya had meant it to be a test, for he never brought up the events of the night again. Having touched her, my curiosity was beginning to transform into an obsession. The worst part was that the obsession was also awash with regret.

Why did I stop when I did? What would you have done?

Wait, don't tell me, for what is to be gained by delving in these matters? It would only serve to make me feel more foolish. If you'd walked away like I did, then I did no better than you'd expect of me. If you had stayed, then I'd begrudge you the opportunity you'd have had.

A few weeks had passed since the last time I had been invited into the mansion. A party to celebrate Amita's birthday was on in full swing at their house.

A tiny diamond sparkled near the centre of her neck. I looked away, what else could I do? Surely, she could tell from my glances what I thought of her? Did she know of the events that had transpired that evening after she had passed out? A hand reached out from behind my shoulder and filled up the glass of wine in front of me. I turned around and stopped the waiter with a glance, "May I have a gin and tonic?"

My mind was both scattered and excited. I found it hard to recollect my thoughts, yet a part of me felt like it was waking up from a slumber and was finally ready to strive for something again. Only, that something was impossible.

It wasn't that I had met Maurya's wife and fallen in love with her at first sight.

What I felt wasn't love. But whatever it was had slowly grown over time. You know how time is, it can be your biggest ally and yet we choose to take conflict with it above most other things.

As I began to stay close to Maurya more and more, our paths began to cross with greater frequency. Usually, it was just a night cap after dinner, then once in a while I began to see her at the casino.

"Are you happy?" I had asked her once.

"I'm more happy than sad."

More happy than sad, more plus than minus, more love than indifference. She leaned forward, and I was filled with a desire to reach out and brush her cheek with my fingers.

I left the table as soon as convention allowed, freeing myself from the writhing tentacles of small talk that slowly squeezed the life out of my mind.

I walked into the library, browsing through the stack of books before singling out a hard-bound copy of Epicurus. The glass clinked as I put it down on a table beside the couch. The silver fluid quivered with displeasure at my decision to divide my attention with the words of a man long dead.

The art of living well, and the art of dying well are one. I distracted myself with prose and the fact that I was separated from Amita by just a few walls weighed less on my mind.

The only time when my attention wavered was when I relieved the glass from the last dregs of liquid. It was with that tinge of wistfulness that I put the book on the table and rescued the empty glass.

I stopped to look at Amita in a group of people standing around a local celebrity. There was an even smattering of men and women around the man, their faces feigning interest. From the looks of it, a pointless question had been asked, following which a well-prepared answer was being delivered with the use of overly heavy prose. Her eyes locked with mine across the space and I quickly walked back to the library.

I had to stop in my tracks as I re-entered the room because a girl now sat in my old spot cradling the book I had been reading. She looked up as I came closer.

"I was reading that."

She smiled as she lowered it into her lap. "I was hoping to find out who would be willing to subject themselves to this while missing out on a party next door."

I stood in front of the couch uncomfortably. Her face seemed familiar, and that smile, though she had a twinkle in the eye that seemed to be out of place. The twinkle – what does a twinkle in somebody's eye look like? I have a hypothesis, when you smile an honest smile, it often reaches into your eyes.

"Would you mind if I get the book back?"

She slowly handed it back without another word, though her eyes reflected that muted glint of amusement we've been talking about, "You probably need it, to resolve the irony you seem to be stuck in."

"What?" I asked.

"Nothing," she said as she rose from the couch and walked towards the bookshelves.

I followed her slow walk across the room, the soft black dress wrapped snugly around her, the hem ending fair few inches above her knees. She was pretty, and yet she could do little to push the image of Amita from my mind.

"Wait," I called after her, "what did you mean when you said I was stuck in an irony?"

She paused by the bookshelves, then walked back to the couch, "Get a girl a drink and I'll tell you."

I looked around helplessly, but the only alcohol in the room was in my glass. I reluctantly offered it to her, which she accepted with a triumphant smile.

Once the ritualistic sacrifice was complete, she settled back and began speaking, "Going by the book you are reading, is it safe to assume that you are not unfamiliar with hedonism?"

Did I know of any other way of life? "No, I'm *not unfamiliar*," I understated.

"Well, considering the company that you are in," she gestured towards the outer room, "I'd have thought that you'd be soaking in the pleasure that the party has to offer, yet you sit here in near seclusion, reading *that book*. Which makes me think that the book is offering you something – a sense of understanding perhaps, maybe you are deriving a measure of calmness?" She followed my face, as if trying to read my reactions.

"Wait. Let's take a quick step back, and pardon me if I'm spending too much time on mundane details," her interest and energy had picked up as she got more entrenched into the conversation.

"The whole concept of pleasure is misunderstood. We seem to associate *hedonism* only with physical joys, *kinetic pleasure* is the term Epicurus used, wasn't it? Sex, food, and indulgence of all kinds as the means of deriving joy. But that isn't the full story, for there is a whole different meaning to pleasure that exists outside of the *kinetic* realm.

"Epicurus's bunch used to call it *Katastematic pleasures*, to achieve a state of serene calmness – Ataraxia – along with near complete absence of pain – Aponia, was to achieve a true lasting form of happiness.

"Our friends in the other room present an opportunity to indulge in immediate *kinetic* fulfilment while the book in your hands has the promise of knowledge that could lead to achieving Katastematic pleasure. You seem to be stuck in between."

She must have seen a hint of admonishment in my eyes, for she stopped to ponder.

"No, you aren't really stuck, are you? You are completely kinetic; your angst probably stems from a different question?" she paused.

"I have no angst," I lied and turned my attention back to the book. It had taken her a few attempts, but she had hit the nail quite quickly on the head. I was as entrenched in kinetic hedonism as anyone could ever be. I indulged myself, and it quenched my proverbial thirst for a bit. *Why was it never enough?*

She must have left the room at some point because the next time she came back to stand in front of me, there was a bottle in her hand.

"I come bearing gifts," she said as she sat. The skirt rode up slightly as she put one leg under the other.

"My name is Maya. You are my brother's new lucky charm?" she asked and answered as she filled my glass.

She was Maurya's sister! That explained the familiar face, and the 'you kiss the ground I walk upon' attitude.

"I'd call him a friend; we like to play together."

"You do not have to justify your relationship with him to me," she said. "Everyone he keeps around himself is there for a purpose, even I."

She pushed her hair to the side, a subtle stone curled around her neck.

"My brother likes to indulge me," she followed my gaze, "he is also very protective."

She leaned over to fill my glass again as it began to run low. "I'll take it that you like to play poker? Would you care to venture a contest?"

“I’d hate to take your money,” I said, but she was already beginning to move from her spot. She stepped beside the table and leaned down. The perfume, the same as Amita’s, washed downwards, a finger reached up and gently grazed my chin.

She leaned forward and planted a suggestive kiss on my lips. “I wasn’t going to wager money.”

23
Caesar

Paradise City
July, 2007

I dreamt of Amita every day and every night. What can a little infatuation do to a man's healthy mind? Maurya must have sensed my discomfort around her and I stopped hanging out at their villa. We spent the evenings playing poker at one of the more privileged tables and then one of his cars would take me home. Life was simpler again, only then there was Maya.

I had been filled with guilt the first time I slept with her. I was afraid that I had betrayed a friend. Was Maurya my friend? No, he wasn't, but I spent most of my waking moments with him. I lived in his house, and I played with his money.

I went as soon as I came that night. Maya couldn't have been happy about it, but I did not look back for a minute as I hurriedly put my clothes back on. "They would've noticed that we are gone," I imagined my voice had been a ragged whisper.

She lit a cigarette as she lay in bed, showing no urgency. She didn't quite share my fear of discovery, why should she have? I had no illusions over whose fault Maurya would see it as.

Three days later she showed up at my door, the now familiar mild amusement playing across her face upon registering the surprise on mine. "How did you find out where I live?"

"This is one of my brother's apartments," she had pushed past me into the living room. "I lived here at one point of time."

Do you think the party at fault changes if the mistake is committed twice? Maya and Amita had the same build, slightly smaller breasts on one, but apart from that, a person who did not want to see their faces could allow himself to mistake one for the other. They dressed similarly, and they smelled the same. I buried my face into her neck as I pushed myself between her thighs, my teeth searching for the nape of her neck, her arms had come up to wrap around me, clinging on to me in a death wish of its own. My body moved with a fervour that was not in my control, pulling at one breast, grabbing at her waist in a desperate attempt to touch something that was beyond my reach. She helped me along, perhaps she understood what I was after, perhaps she was reaching for something herself. We pushed against each other's bodies until we could push no more.

She was *a* biter. Like a cat trying to find her way around my body by biting me all over, grabbing a little skin at my chest between her teeth and then alternating between sucking at it and kissing it, first gently then hard till it hurt, leaving a trail of hickeys behind. The darkness of my skin hid them as best as was possible, but some would inadvertently stand out.

I closed my eyes as she pulled my face up towards herself and surrendered myself to a fervent kiss. Till the time that I opened my eyes, I thought I was with Amita. I could hardly separate the two anymore.

Maya would drop by unannounced, and I would let her in. Why could I not have slept with any of the other hundred thousand girls in the city? Why choose to betray Maurya in this manner? Perhaps because he had denied me the joy of loving Amita? But hadn't the man offered his wife to me?

After those first few meetings, it became apparent that I was but a game to her, a way of getting back at her brother for some wrong perhaps.

Even on the days that I'd try to resist, she'd notice that I was slow to respond and pushed me along with a few tense touches and a kiss here and there. I'd close my eyes and submit, and she'd win. But did she know that she was losing too? My mind refused her, but my body wanted her body. But here's the pickle, and here is what I'll pin this on if I'm ever questioned – every time I closed my eyes, I thought of Amita.

Maya would walk around the house naked or in her tiny underwear. The sensual curves of her body were a slap in my face, a sign of my weakness. "Never again," I'd whisper, but that would only last till the time that she'd climb back into bed with me a few seconds later.

24
Amita

Paradise City
July, 2007

Jules was a quiet boy. Then again, how old could he have been. He was a youngling, certainly no older than twenty-fivc. Proximity with Maurya got him into many places which might well have evaded him otherwise, but then, he handled it well.

I must admit, I was worried about him. Why should a boy so young look so desolate? Especially someone who had everything that he did.

I found him in a booth staring into a glass of bubbly, one of his fingers moved lazily on his phone. The tousled hair had finally given up against the fervent forces of his hand pulling at it in one direction or another and lay lazily the wrong way. The green of his eyes looked a solemn dark brown in the light. He would turn out to be a handsome man if he could ever get over that insipid boredom.

"Are you happy?" he had asked me once.

Wait, have I not introduced myself? What folly. I am Amita. I used to be a lawyer at some point. I still am, but the nature of my work has changed drastically.

"Yes," I answered, "for the most part."

"What does that mean?"

"I don't know," I said, "perhaps that I'm more happy than sad."

I continued when Jules didn't respond, "It may be vain to try and encompass all states of your life under the blanket of one word. Why should a minute extract of the English language be enough to describe your complete existence?"

"But we must, mustn't we? Otherwise, how will we know if we are doing it right?"

"Doing what right?"

"Living."

"Oh, young boy, what brought about this train of thought?"

"Nothing," he said. "I have some time to think, so why not think about ... existence." He sounded disappointed with himself, as if by bringing up this question his brain had somehow betrayed him.

He picked up his glass and emptied it.

"You know, Maurya has a theory. Would you like to hear it?"

He shrugged.

"He believes that life, for all intents and purposes, can have no inherent meaning. Everything that we do is nothing but a digression, playing or praying, drinking, eating, sleeping – everything we do is an act of taking attention away from the passage of time. Even the simple act of meditating and taking control of your mind is a digression, because in trying to force yourself to not think about something, you are in effect thinking about not thinking."

The waiter brought forward a cocktail and propped it in front of him. Jules gave him a thankful smile, and in that innocent gratitude, I saw a young boy. The smile dissolved and the boy vanished, and the bored man was back in front of me.

"That sounds... depressing?"

I couldn't help but shrug, "Maybe."

We sat in silence for a little while.

"You should talk more about it with him. I think Boy has probably heard it a million times."

"Which one is Boy?"

"The tall brooding one," she pointed at a man across the bar to me. "He is Maurya's number one guy. Or well, used to be. He spends most of time painting now."

For a moment it seemed as if Jules's interest was mildly piqued, "Hmmph," was all he could muster as a response.

"You should talk to him sometime," I said as I got up to leave.

"Maybe I will," I heard him say.

25
Caesar

Paradise City
July, 2008

All humans are thieves at heart. It took me two years in Paradise City to realise that we are programmed to grab and take for ourselves what we can. We seek refuge in the safety of the rules that the cumulative has set around us. You must forgive me here if I presume too much about the world. All my experiments have only one subject, me, and I have no choice but to project on the world what I see in myself.

Maya took me to her home one night. She lived in another little palace in Maurya's tiny kingdom. The apartment was inside out. The walls on the outside were all glass, and the ones on the inside had plants everywhere. We were on the thirtieth floor. The place had no balconies but at one point the marble of the floor merged into glass and extended outwards over thirty floors of nothingness.

I would like to tell you that I fucked her brains out on that glass floor and as we both orgasmed, I looked down into the eyes of death with its salivating fangs waiting for the fall that would surely have come had it not been for the resistance of the thin transparent layer of metamorphosed silica.

I would like to tell you all of it, but I would be lying, my knees slipped and slid at first. And only when I had managed to secure a tenuous grasp on the exasperatingly smooth surface did I realise that under the pretext of saving me, the unrelenting glass was using my weight as a weapon to attack my soft kneecaps.

"When I suggested that we do this, I thought it was sexy," I muttered to Maya, "but this is just plain fucking uncomfortable."

She finally flipped me over and took control. *She* fucked my brains out and screamed into the expanse while I tried to hide my shame from an unseasonal bougainvillea.

Almost like a ritual, we cuddled for a while before I dressed to leave. "I think I'm falling for you, Jules," I heard her say from behind me. I wavered, delaying eye contact for as long as possible as my brain tried to think of an appropriate response. She was gorgeous like that, the white bed sheet flowing over her thighs bunched over her breasts gently fighting with her dishevelled hair. "I know that you don't feel the same way. I think you should leave Paradise."

"What?"

For the first time in our time together, I could see an expression other than mirth or lust on her face. It reminded me of my sister, and the perennial anguish in her eyes. "You don't need to get it, just go away."

"I'll think about it," I said as I left the apartment.

My descent was sudden.

It started off with that brief conversation and Maya's words attached themselves to the feelings of resentment which had been festering within me. Maurya had shown me nothing but kindness since beating me in that game two years ago and being in his employment had improved my bank account's health to no end. But the more kindness he showed me, the more I hated him.

I lost some house money that evening. It came mostly from a feeling of not caring about winning or losing sprinkled with a dash of arrogance.

That evening was followed by a bad month where I ended up losing Maurya a few million euros.

After a particularly unsatisfactory day he invited me home. “I think you should take a break.”

I had expected anger and found warmth instead. “Jules, you’ve been playing relentlessly for two years now, and some mental fatigue is bound to set in.”

“I’m fine.”

“It affects all of us, you don’t need to feel bad about it. You are running a marathon at sprinting pace.”

“I said I’m fine.”

He looked at me with a troubled expression.

“Can I do anything else for you?”

“Yes,” I said in exasperation.

“Name it.”

“I want to sleep with Amita.”

The rush of adrenaline came back like an old friend. I had missed it. So much.

He paused for only a second before nodding. “I’ll make it happen. We are having a party over the weekend; you can stay back at the end.”

“I want her to be awake.”

He nodded and smiled, “Of course, that is how we’ll do it.”

His words gave me pause. A moment of anger had put words on an indecent request and a moment of empathy had led to its acceptance.

“Why would you be ok with this?”

“Why wouldn’t I?”

“She is your wife. Don’t you have some sense of possession?”

He actually laughed. “I possess her in ways that you can’t imagine, as she possesses me. This is just sex. We have but one life; she should be able to derive whatever joy she wants from it."

"I want you to stay away from the tables for the next few days," he said. "Take some time off, detox, stay away from alcohol, hit the spa, workout, get massages and rest."

I nodded and agreed, but the next day I went back to the tables anyway. This time I lost in defiance. I folded with a full house at hand because I could. Maurya may be a king in the city, but he wouldn't rule my life.

If I try now to explain the root of it all, I'd say that the violence that I had suppressed in my head for all this time was coming up in the form of a stubborn contempt. Most of that contempt was for myself for I had begun to see the world around me in myself. The world I had hated had become me, or perhaps more truthfully, the transformation was the other way around.

Maurya was furious. I suppose it was more because I didn't do his bidding and less because of the money he lost. By the evening I had an ultimatum at my door. Stay away from the tables or I'd be forcefully removed from the city.

I'm tempted to think that this was what my subconscious had been angling for all the time. I didn't have the courage to quit the city so my brain conceived a series of actions that would have Maurya fire me instead. I know the truth though. It was nothing but impetuous malice on my part that made me lose money in those games because I didn't go back to the tables after his final warning.

26
Caesar

Paradise City
July, 2008

I haven't been entirely honest about a few things here.

Maya was a happy girl, but not in an easy-going, comfortable about how life was turning out way; she was happy in a fearful-to-be sad way. Something in her past might have haunted her, maybe her angst was purely existential, but the result at the end was that she couldn't bear to be sad.

Her mind wasn't at peace and most of the time her body could not keep up with her expectations. So, she made up for these with healthy doses of MDMA. The surge of serotonin would bring with it newfound and often misplaced empathy inside her. And she'd hold on to me as if it provided her with more joy than anything else in the world.

The serotonin surge was followed by a dangerous dip where she'd be wracked with a nervous anxiety and be suspicious of everything around her.

The fix was usually easy, for she would do one of three things: recipe number one would be to sleep it out. A long nap filled with anxious dreams was the first answer. At times when she was too wound up for this to make a difference, she'd indulge instead in frantic sex. This was largely for my benefit, but on occasion I had to wonder if she was truly there with me, but then who was I to question her? I'd just quietly close my eyes and imagine I was with Amita. The third answer was always getting right back on the pill. If her body hadn't recovered well enough to support her with the serotonin she needed, she'd make up for it by adding a hundred milligrams of some sort of unprescribed medication to her diet.

Lo and behold, our happy-go-lucky princess would be back before we knew it. I hung out with her a lot more than we've let on so far. Perhaps every other evening after I was done playing.

We never went to Maurya's clubs in the city, or any other place where we'd be easily visible to the public eye. Under the upward layer of sophistication and glamour lay a noisier and chaotic underbelly. These were usually house bars that moved from one location to another, small confines that housed a familiar group of fifty or so people locked in a pseudo embrace with the music and each other. The rooms had an energy of their own, as one, it went up and down together, as the music became frenetic, the dancing became frantic, followed by a wave of confused calmness, repeating itself over and over again till the evening slowly petered out.

For some reason, she seemed to be more at peace with me at these mobile clubs than she was at her place or mine.

I woke up to the sound of breaking glass one morning after one of these parties. She had broken the coffee pot and was now agonising over mopping up the brown fluid that was quickly getting absorbed by the pale white carpet.

"Pick out the glass first, or else you'll cut your hand on it," I said as I knelt down to help her clean up. Her bloodshot eyes screamed an accusation at me, as if I had conspired with the pot to cause her this distress. Anger seemed to be bubbling up inside her.

She gave the carpet another look of dismay before throwing the chunks of glass back on the floor and heading back to the bedroom.

I retrieved the broken glass. I tried to throw some salt on the coffee stains to see if it would help at all. But as it turned out, coffee doesn't react with salt the same way as wine does.

A part of me wanted to let myself out right then, just so I wouldn't have to deal with it all.

I wouldn't win any awards for boyfriend of the year, that much I know, but it wasn't as if she was actively fighting her demons. The more I tried to invest myself in her worries, the more risk I ran of being consumed in it.

I stopped to look at her face as I retrieved my clothes from the dresser. She had drifted off to sleep again and serenity had returned to her being. A pool of blood around her hand caught my attention a lazy second later. I stupidly examined her wrists, but they were thankfully scratch less, the damage was on her palm where she tightly clutched onto a piece of glass from the coffee pot. I had to prise off her fingers one by one before I could get it out of her hand. The wound wasn't deep, at least not the one on her hand.

I wasn't completely irresponsible. I used her phone to send a message to her maid before heading out. I would have thought that perhaps we could have healed each other, but her malady was different from mine. Whatever tormented her had its meaning closer to the physical world; what tormented me was a growing sense of doubt in the meaning of the world itself. I fled from the scene of crime, like a thief who had come to rob a house and stumbled upon a murder.

Rest assured that when she turned up at my place a few days later, I didn't have the heart to keep her out. We were back to our old games soon enough and neither one of us referred to the bandage on her hand to each other or anyone else.

27
Caesar

Paradise City
July, 2008

I ignored Maya at the party. It wasn't a conscious decision; my mind was preoccupied, and for a moment, I couldn't think. The glass of wine was untouched. On any other day, I would have dived into it with a fervour that I reserve for the poker tables, tonight the brain didn't want to function in the same manner.

I turned my head around to look at Amita and caught her staring at me. What game was this really? Did he invite men at random into his bedroom or was this a privilege reserved for a few people? I might have desired it less if the prize wasn't exclusive.

Later that evening, we had retired to their suite on the second floor overlooking the gardens. I kissed Amita, but something was missing, my fingers trailed across the arm as my lips prodded at hers, not unkindly, just insistently. She responded with an adequate amount of passion; she was not emphatic, nor desperate, just there.

Maurya sat in an armchair, quietly observing us as I tentatively pressed against the boundaries of intimacy before eventually breaching them. At any moment I expected him to spring up from his chair and pull me away from his precious wife. One of my hands had found its way to the bottom of her dress and I slowly slid under the hem, grabbing lightly at the skin, caressing the soft flesh of her thighs while the other hand now moved inwards from her arm towards her left breast. I broke away from the kiss for a minute to trace her neck with my lips.

"Is there no way to get inside this thing?" I asked.

"You need to take it off." I looked into her eyes, and it seemed as if desire had finally awakened inside her.

"Do you want me to?" I asked her.

She nodded, "Very much."

I slid off her dress and something within me snapped. Her eyes closed as I kissed my way down to her stomach. The mechanical side of me had taken control.

My fingers went underneath the waistbands, and I pulled her underwear off. My tongue traced a line along her labia. The movement made her quiver, and a hand came forward to grasp the back of my head, pushing me further between her legs. I took the opportunity to pleasure her for a while before pulling her legs over my shoulders and entering her in a swift motion.

I hid my nose in her neck, a desire finally satiated, a sense of jubilation materialised somewhere at this new-found possession and soon *that* jubilation overpowered *all passion*. I basked in the feeling for a few seconds.

The feeling did not last. All of a sudden, a vast emptiness surrounded me, and I lost all sense of time or place. I finally opened my eyes and looked up at Amita. I realised that this meant nothing at all, the chase had gone too far till the time that pleasure was now meaningless. I pulled out of her in a rush and pushed myself off the bed, horrified at myself.

My eyes could still trace a shadow of me curled between her legs, pushing at her out of practice. I could see my head bent above her face, my lips a few millimetres apart, my gyrating hips moving backward and forward with a practised fervour. Slowly the image faded, and I saw the surprised woman sitting up in bed, looking down at me on the floor.

"It's all a digression," I finally said as my head cleared. "Isn't that what you said the other day?"

She had grabbed a bed cover protectively to cover her body, but did not say a word.

"It doesn't matter that we digress Julius, it matters how we digress. That is what you haven't properly figured out," Maurya said from behind me.

"What do you mean?"

"Have you ever wondered why you are at peace playing the cards? It's because you are a hero there, you are the best you know, you've spent years mastering the art of reading people and paper – on the poker tables, you can digress heroically. Out here, you digress mindlessly, and that serves to give you no pleasure."

"I don't understand."

He smiled, "Once you've tasted the pleasure of being a hero, all other pleasures are tasteless."

"So, what's the point? I should live on the tables all my life?" I asked.

"No, just that you need to find ways to be more heroic in other things that you do."

"Life is radioactive, a net negative, every moment you expend a bit of your life and die just a little. In a meaningless digression, that bit just fizzles out for no good use. But when you digress heroically, you have the opportunity to compound the energy you expended into something more," he continued.

"It's an insatiable quest though, I must warn you, the desire to constantly fight the decline and constantly grow to be more than your earlier self."

This was too much for my poor mind to fathom at that moment. "I need to get out of here."

"You are fighting to be human, Julius," Maurya's voice echoed behind me, "When your real quest is to be a hero."

28
Caesar

Paradise City
July, 2008

Was it an instance with a twist of fate, or is all fate twisted itself?

The first time I had entered the city seemed to be a lifetime away now. I was penniless and dangerous, and now I had slept with the queen and the crowned princess.

Maya put a finger on my lips one evening and slid in a small flat pill inside my mouth. I sat and waited for something to happen. We were a small group of people in the room; the party was just starting out. A projector was throwing a kaleidoscope of lights on the wall and I forced myself to focus on the patterns to see if it triggered a mental response of some sort.

"Don't force it. It will happen when it happens." She kissed me gently.

"Should I take another pill?" I asked her. "That one was either too little or fake."

"No, give it time. It needs time to work. It comes together in a slight wave. Once it dissolves into your bloodstream, you are greeted by a burst of comfort and happiness, followed by a trough of calm nothingness. Taking another pill would not necessarily intensify those sensations; it will merely put your body on two such waves."

"Sounds good to me! Shouldn't I just take 5 pills and put myself on 5 waves?"

She laughed. "You can't stay high all the time, love. You need to come down. There is no running away from it. The higher you try to be, the deeper the desolation waiting for you. Don't think about it too much, just give it a few minutes."

She kissed me again.

We haven't spoken enough about the events of the recent past with Amita and Maurya.

I desired Amita, as much as a person desires to possess something impossible. But when I finally had her, the thrill of achievement did not live up to the joy of wanting it.

To live under the shadow of a constant desire, isn't that the ideal life then? But to not grasp something that you've finally achieved is plain madness.

Should I have pulled my hand away at the last instant so that I could have lived with the craving for a little longer? How many times could I have done that before it transcended into madness?

These are questions I cannot answer, unfortunately.

But being a hero sounded like a lot of work. How else could I digress? The whole subject sent my brain into a spiral. Could I choose a life of un-heroic digression then?

Maya had most certainly not imbibed her brother's ideals. She lived a far simpler life than her brother. Get drunk, screw around, pop a pill here or there – whatever it took to get to the other side. Perhaps she had understood the tirelessness required to continue to satiate a hero's desire and chosen a different path.

Sometime over this last year or so of digressing together, we had become friends. We both knew that the other person battled with questions of their own, and while neither had the desire to pick up the burden of the other's discomfort, we made room for it in our lives.

Maya must have seen the slow change come over my bearing. She hugged me so hard that I felt that I could feel her heart beating through her chest. I kissed the top of her head, and I could feel her smile.

I felt a sudden urge to come clean. Surely, she could find it within herself to forgive me. In a moment of clarity, I began pouring my heart out. Every little story, from the day that I had stepped into the city spilled out, every feeling, every instance of madness. She listened to me with a serene calmness, even when I told her that I had lusted after Amita. She listened to me with an understanding smile. I told her that none of it mattered, that Amita never mattered, that all I desired now was Maya.

She laughed, not unkindly, "You don't desire me."

"But I do, I've never felt this comfort that I feel now."

"That, quite unfortunately, is how you are expected to feel when you take Ecstasy. This isn't a true feeling, Jules."

I would have to admit to you that a bit of content disappointment followed.

"Let's go back to my place."

It felt as if I was seeing her for the first time when I looked into her eyes. I held on to her arms before allowing myself to fall into the warmth of her body. We clung to each other for a long time. I must have drifted off at some point because it was a distinctive feel of something cold sliding along my stomach that woke me up.

She was straddling me, and she held a long knife in her hand, the tip of which rested sharply on my skin. "I could tell that you were never truly *there*, but to think of her while you slept with me is a betrayal. As if she hadn't taken enough from me already."

"This has to end Jules," she said.

"It has ended..." I began to whisper, but a gasp escaped me as the knife entered the side of my abdomen before I could finish my sentence.

Maya leaned down to kiss me as she pushed harder on the knife, "I told you that I was falling for you." A tear trickled down from her eyes and fell on my face. Her wet eyes blurred her vision and she started wiping the tears off with one hand. I used that moment of weakness to push her off myself and slid out of the bed. My motion had pushed the knife free, and it fell to the floor with a guilty clang. I pushed past her and ran out of the bedroom, slamming the door shut behind me.

I couldn't leave right away. I could hear her sobbing on the other side of the door as I stemmed the blood with a piece of cloth from the kitchen. I would live, the knife hadn't gone in too deep before I had managed to push her off me.

I slid down in front of the door and listened to her. Her inconsolable sobbing tore at me. Now that the waves of MDMA had worn off, I could sense the distant desolation approaching. But through that desolation, I knew what I had said to Maya the night before could be true. If only we tried to make it true. Could that be our collective digression? I heard her walk to the door and the gentle thud indicated that she had claimed a spot on the floor on the other side of the thin wood.

Soon, the sobbing stopped. "Maya?" I turned the handle on the door and tried to go back in, but she had locked it from the other side.

"Maya, open the door."

A gentle murmur answered back.

"Maya, let me in. I want to talk to you; we need to set this straight. I was wrong. Just let me in and let me say all this to you while I can look at you."

A soft sob answered in return.

"Maya, open the door."

It was only when I saw the trickle of blood from under the door that I remembered that I had left the knife inside the room when I ran.

Interlude

I
Victoria

Several cities in France & Spain
August, 2011

The first hundred times that I called August he did not answer; my next hundred calls went to voice mail. After that the operator just told me that the phone number was not in use.

I looked up his friends on social media, but they hadn't heard from him for years. At one point he had chosen a time to walk away from his life and apparently, he had never looked back. He was trying to do it again with me.

As the futility of all my actions mocked me, I sat at home and sulked. Both Amir and I knew that we were done, but neither of us was prepared to walk away.

I sat there on the front porch trying to remember every moment we spent together, piecing together every memory bit by bit, trying to pick up hints from our conversations.

I sense a little judgment, maybe it's all just coming from me and not you. But let me take a moment to justify my actions anyway.

I know I said not too long ago that Amir was the person I loved the most, but I loved August too. I had loved Amir because of how he made me feel about life. But at some point, I began to love August more because of how he made me feel about myself. All those things had existed all this time, but my perspective changed slightly, and it turned my whole life around. I was a spoilt brat, but I knew what I wanted more than anything else in this world and that was to be with August.

I traced out every story that tied him to a place, and then created a map for myself. Once I was done, half of the continent lay in front of me. There was just one place to start, wasn't it. The place he loved the most.

Amir's last embrace was warm and forgiving. Was it an indication to stay? I couldn't tell, for a moment I was afraid that he would put it into words. Mercifully, he didn't, and I walked away without a promise to him.

I landed in Paris that evening. I didn't have a plan. I hoped to spend my days in a coffee shop and my evenings in a bar somewhere till he turned up. A week turned into a month, a month into two, he didn't turn up at any of those hours that I sat at the back at Angelina's, nibbling on crumbs of Le Mont-Blanc and sipping my chocolate chaud.

I walked along Rue Mouffetard, only occasionally glancing through the glass windows of the hundred or so boutiques on the street. I ate a customary taco before stepping through the back door into Candelaria. I waited with a Margarita in my hand, but he wouldn't come. Those endless walks along the streets of Marais, and the jaunts along the Seine. I even stepped inside Le Notre Dame at one point and prayed. What could I promise a god who'd help me find the love of my life? Faith maybe? I could start believing in a god that brought me face to face with August.

I listened to unfulfilled poets sing their ballads at Le chat noir. I did everything he loved, and he never came, so I moved on.

For a while I spent time loitering around, one week walking back and forth over the Saône in Lyon, another ambling across

La Rambla in Barcelona, then moving from one Catalan village to another. I realised that I was going around in circles when I ended up in a small Pintxo bar in San Sebastian one fine evening. The name of the street was 31 de Agosto, it literally translates into the 31st of August. A photographed copy of the 'The Storming of San Sebastian' by Denis Dighton hung on the wall. It told the story of an unforgettable day at the end of August in 1813 when the British and Portuguese troops finally broke through the French defences to lay claim to the city that had been Napoleon's last stand in the Iberian Peninsula. They had besieged the city for the whole summer, and when the chance to finally lay down their claim arrived, they decided to raze it to the ground instead. The victors kept the city burning for several days, till the only stones that survived unburnt lay on the street I sat on.

Not every story has to be a metaphor, sometimes stories are just stories. But this one isn't. I have a revelation, and this is the most important thing I'll ever tell you, so read carefully.

Epicurus said that happiness can only be achieved through a combination of a state where pain was absent – aponia, and complete freedom from mental distress was achieved – ataraxia. In the recent past I had chosen to throw my belief behind love, and that had brought me both physical pain and mental distress. Love was the exact antithesis of happiness as Epicurus defined it. Was love my destruction?

I spent a hundred days and a hundred nights in paradise city to no avail. I couldn't find the man, but I did pick up some more stories. Not many people remembered him, but once in a while, a hint of recognition would flower on someone's face, "The prince of the fallen chips, the one who must not be blamed, the man with the lost ending. I thought he was dead, no? So many loose endings going around."

"One says that he messed around with Maurya's sister who had him killed in a village by the coast in Italia some years ago, while another theme is that he didn't really die there – he swam across a river to hide from the men who hunted him and then vanished. Who knows which story is true? Maybe Maurya himself, but no one else. Maybe we are talking about different people after all." Not all of the stories added up, actually none of them did. But I struggled on with whatever little thread I had to guide me.

I called Maurya at the hotels he ran and visited the clubs he owned. On occasion, I managed to get a glimpse of him, but his guards wouldn't let me past. Maurya proved to be no easier to get hold of than August had been. For reasons that were hard to fathom, he didn't want to give me an audience. I tried to sit in on his games, but he'd leave as soon as I was allowed on to a table. I did the only thing a sane and simple-minded girl could have done in this scenario. I climbed over the wall and jumped into his mansion one fine full moon night.

What's the worst that could happen, right? I repeated to myself a few times and took the leap. Unfortunately, they caught me three minutes into my little adventure, and I was shown fairly unceremoniously into a dank and dark room. Was I worried in there? No, not really! I mean I had only tried to sneak into the house of a mobster with a penchant for angry outbursts. I didn't think it through.

Imagine my surprise then when the man who walked in through the door turned out to be Amir.

"You have to stop asking around about August in these parts," he said.

I have to admit, seeing the old love of my life walk in through the door threw me off balance and I didn't have an opportunity to spout neither my lies nor my excuses.

He slipped an envelope across the table, "This is where you'll find him," he spoke softly. I couldn't sense any resentment in his voice, nor was there any sign of reproach at how things had ended.

I carefully picked up the envelope. "How..." I began, but he cut me short.

"You should go now," he said. As if on cue, a man entered the room. "Max'll show you out."

I wanted to ask him how he'd been, but he didn't give me a chance. But he was Amir, what else could he be but fine. Amir was indestructible, the irony of the situation wasn't lost on me. I had left him to search for August when he had the answer all this time. The mystery of the situation wasn't lost on me either. How had he known?

August would eventually fill in all the blanks in the story. At that time, I ran for him.

***

I tracked him down to a bordello in Granada. He was eyeing a woman in a deliberately short skirt with a deep cake of rouge on her cheeks.

"Is that what you are into?" I asked as I slunk into the seat next to him. "I mean, she's gorgeous and everything. But I thought you still had some fight and charm left in yourself to pick up a drunk girl in a bar like a proper gentleman."

He didn't show any uncertainty towards my presence, as if someone had alerted him to my arrival. "I don't sleep with them, I just like to come here and look," he said finally.

"Why?"

"Because... why are you here?" he finally asked.

I shrugged.

"You shouldn't have come, now I'll have to leave this town."

"Where are you going?"

"Nowhere, everywhere, somewhere. I've been stuck for a while and haven't found an answer yet. I'm afraid, I try to run away from fear, and it turns out that I end up running towards it. I've become a digressionist."

"A digressionist?"

"I take pleasure from devoting myself to any pursuit, just so I wouldn't focus on what's at the end."

"I sense a bit of Amir in your words," I said. "You know that he usually doesn't know what he's talking about. What else is there?"

"Imperishable happiness."

"There is no such thing."

"How would you know?"

"Not through proof, but through argument. Nothing is imperishable, nothing at all, everything dies. Even the strongest of the feelings change."

"This world is imperishable."

"Is it?"

"The universe? Surely that is imperishable."

"Perhaps, but now you risk losing yourself in abstraction like all those thinkers who you so idolise. Wouldn't it be meaningful to master digression before you are ready to move further?"

"I don't know how?"

I reached forward to grab his hand, "We'll figure it out." I had kissed him once before, but this was different. Now we didn't have the spectre of Amir hanging over us. I softly pressed my lips on to his.

"We'll figure it out?" he asked me.

"At least some of it."

***

"I found this book in your room after you left." We had been driving for a few days. August had been surprised to find all my stuff in the car. I told him I did not believe in half measures. "There was a dog-eared page in there somewhere, which spoke of recurrence. Speak of it to me."

"Nietzsche," he began, "spoke of eternal recurrence, that existence recurs in an infinite cycle as energy and matter transform over time. The idea was not unique to Nietzsche; the wheel of time in Hinduism and Buddhism believes similarly that time is cyclical. Thus, the life we are living right now, as it is, will recur, back to this moment. Over and over. A thousand times, a million times."

"Like an hourglass flipped back and forth."

"Like an hourglass... The question he wanted you to ask is this: if this moment was to happen a thousand, a million times over, would you still take the same actions? Would you be willing to live life as it is over and over again? And if not, why would you continue persisting in this state even once?"

We drove in silence for a while as we both pondered over what he had said.

"May I ask you a question?" he asked after a while, "Why did you leave Amir?"

"Your answer preceded your question."

A glimmer of recognition and hope had entered his eyes. He nodded and continued to drive on.

II
Octavia

Somewhere unknown
August, 2015

I remember a time when we were young and restless. Jules and I, we'd run around the house from seven in the morning till five in the afternoon, and then we'd run some more. He'd follow me around, I, Jules and the dog, one behind the other, someone in front of someone else, drawing imaginary circles in the sand.

As some people would often say, we were happier then when the times were simpler. But if simplicity was the sole virtue of happiness, then my fate right now would be ideal.

I asked for some vodka today and they gave me a generous glass. I should stop being surprised by these trifles. It wasn't much, but it would have to be enough. I dropped three of the pills in it and swallowed them? How long ago was it? Fifteen minutes? Twenty? It is hard to tell. I should take the rest soon, lest the effect of the first three is compromised before the others kick in.

Having a brother close to you in age is both good and bad. I shared a level of closeness with him that I have seldom found elsewhere. Even when we were no longer close, and I had room in my life for more people. I could never connect with others in the same way. He was also my biggest competitor and critic. I loved him for a bit, before he went away and became someone else.

Pill four and pill five, how are you doing friends? Perhaps it'll help if I close my eyes while I wait? Would you know?

Thinking about my brother brings up the faces, this isn't ideal; it seems that they'll haunt me as they chase me out of the door. His face, such difference between the boy he was and the man he became. Many people would have found ways to blame it on the family or on money. He wanted for neither of those; he just craved for his highs.

I'll sandwich my irony between pill six and pill seven. Do I sense my heart slowing? I should just hold my breath, I could forget that I need to start breathing again?

Before we continue though, may I ask you for the tiniest of favours? Can you put on some music for me? Do not pass this off as words on paper, consider it as a request. If you have something close by – put on Nocturnal by Benjamin Britten.

If this life was a gift from god, then in squandering it in the face of suffering is wrong. The theological aspect of the case sentences this as a crime, but I'm an atheist.

How about I come at this from the point of a libertarian? I have complete ownership over my body, my labour, and the fruit of my labours. I can do with all these as I please, thus is my right if thus were to be my will.

If I were to test my actions against the consequentialist framework to assess if this was the right decision, I would have to go over who my actions might affect and in what way, positive or negative. If me taking those last few pills were to leave a child unfed or a senescent uncared for, then this would be a mistake. But I can assure you that I leave no incomplete painful stories as such behind me. The net sum of all outcomes here is positive, as it ends my suffering, and it frees my captors of their distasteful job.

But what of the ways of Kant? He who thought that life possessed an unconditional, incomparable, and implicit worth, and that the only way to live was to live with the dignity that a gift such as this demanded. If killing myself now was to deny myself of this dignity, then what I'm doing is a huge folly.

It is two for and two against, and I have a fifth reason of my own to add to this equation. What of freedom? The right to freedom cannot be contested. Not by religion, not by a government, not by a philosopher long dead. In a place where my freedom is threatened, where I'm a captive of my suffering with no apparent way out. Does it make sense for me to prolong this further? To what end and to whose gain?

Pill eight and pill nine, you are my only hope for freedom. Do not let me down dear lovers. Watch over me till the end of this prose, will you? But promise me to go over to the next part of the story.

Pill ten.

III
Maurya and all of his unfortunate friends

India
1980 - 1998

Almost everyone who knew Amir, called him *Boy*.

All families become rich or poor as the tide of what the world values shift. So we cannot be sure of when Amir's foremothers and fathers had devolved into poverty, but what we can be sure of is that he was born in the poorest of poor families in a village of boys. He was the second child in a rare family with an older sister. The land in the village was fertile but the rewards were owned by one family while the rest worked long hours for the promise of the landowners' mercy and justice. It wasn't to be long when Amir's father would end his miserable life through continuous abuse of his organs at the hands of cheap liquor. Mother and sister continued to toil in the fields to bring home wheat enough for a meal or two at a time. Even through the painful times the small family of three managed a smile or two. At night under the skies, they'd often dream of a job in the city for two women, and a school for Amir where he'd pick up the skills needed to transform his life and theirs.

Amir remembered the night when a man forced himself into their home and asked mother to dig up all her meagre savings. He pointed his knife at her precious son as he ordered her to bring out all the little pennies she had being setting aside. She hadn't fought, it wasn't much money anyway.

Over the years, he had learned to block out the memories of his childhood to the point that now he couldn't tell the difference between the truth and his own imagination. But whenever he closed his eyes, he could remember that the colour of misfortune had been stark. One evening, some men had come to take away his sister; maybe they took her to the place where all the other girls went. It was a village of boys after all.

That night Amir heard his mother's gentle sobs that belied the leathery smile that she had been greeting him with every morning. He had heard her cry many a times before, but there was something different about that evening. Her body shook as she fought and lost to each sob, the sound of her cry deeply suppressed and yet slowly increasing but stopping short as her lungs finally ran out of breath.

Amir would see many a joyous day in his life, unlike his mother or sister, but that desolation would never leave him. No matter where he went in life, it would stay forever, safe at the back of his mind – like a north star always ready to guide him back to the sorrow that was written in his destiny. His mother had sold everything of value in their house and assigned him to one of the men travelling to the city to work in Maurya's father's construction projects. She asked him to make five promises:

"Work hard in the city," she said.

"Take care of yourself," she said.

"Don't be naughty," she said.

"Make some friends," she said.

"Never come back to the village," she said.

He would go on to break one of the promises, the rest he kept.

The village had taught him the skill of being deferent to everyone. When he came to the city, he realised that this was a tad unnecessary and that he only needed to be deferent to the folks more powerful than him. After spending some years in the city, he realised another important fact – that if he was deferent to the most powerful folks and managed to win their favour, then he didn't need to show deference to anyone else.

Winning favour with the powerful folks was hardly easy, but this was a boy who had suffered much and lost a lot. They sent him to throw a rock into a window of a house, and he did it with diligence, without asking questions. He ran when he was asked to run. On the rare occasions when people managed to catch him, he learned how to bite; it worked impressively well. He took the knife when it was finally offered and didn't think twice before sinking it into somebody's flesh. The first person who died of his hand was an accident. Amir had only intended to stab him, but he had struggled and fought back, and the knife had ended up puncturing a major artery in his throat. In a life that had seen a horror or two, this was another disappointing anecdote on existence. People could die of a whisker of a cut and for not much of a reason, apparently.

When Maurya's father died and the business was sold off, Amir took the opportunity to switch employers, and quite fortuitously, ended up in Dhanraj Nanda's employment. He saw reflections of his village in Nanda's small kingdom, and it might have bothered him more had he not been one of the more powerful men in Nanda's army of mercenaries.

By the time Vishnu finally sought him out a few years later, he had developed quite a reputation among the workers. He was known to be a fair person; if he could get away with a slap or two, that's what he'd do. If a cut was necessary to send a message, he'd keep it shallow and close to the fleshy muscles so as not to cut through any organs. He never killed a person unless he expressly wanted to. Vishnu both understood and appreciated these subtleties. It was after all an art to do what Amir did.

Amir had only seen a world where the more powerful used the less powerful like a resource, the world had deemed him only worthy of being an object and he had fashioned himself into a weapon. But Vishnu and Maurya's approach to dealing with the poor stymied him.

"Building cheap housing would tie the workers down to the place, in an industry where people tend to move around from project to project, this is a great way to keep them near," he had heard Vishnu say to Maurya. "Plus the development land would practically be free, and we'll deduct a rent from their salaries in perpetuity that will make us back the money in less than ten years."

It was a good deal from the sound of it.

What happened next completely blew Amir's mind. Maurya and Vishnu went as far ahead as building a school for the workers' children along with a small hospital, "Let's give them a taste of a lifestyle that can only come with setting roots in a place and then they'll never dream of leaving," Vishnu said as Maurya listened.

What they did next sowed some seeds of loyalty in Amir's mind for the first time. "Let's find a way to teach them something more; there is a lot of stuff happening in the west that we can learn from. We'll never get the same number of people to work for us as Dhanraj, so we need to make do with less. Let us try and offer a way to specialise our workers so that they can be better at what they do."

"What about the women?" Maurya had asked.

"The wives?"

"Yes, it is easy for people to leave one job and move away, but if they have two jobs in the family from one employer, it should double the incentive to stay. Some of those workers keep getting drunk and creating trouble. If we manage to make the wives financially independent, it might empower them to keep their husbands in check."

As they fought the battles outside, little by little they used the resources and people at their disposal to build foundations for their company, and pretty soon the small *city in the city* that developed was locked in a virtuous cycle.

***

On the other side of Maurya and Vishnu's little war, Maya battled a whole different turmoil of her own. After years of feeling lost, for a brief while she had felt like she was beginning to find herself. But that feeling had evaporated with the events of the day in the hospital when she had realised that she now had romantic feelings for the man she couldn't recognise as her brother.

In the days following Maya's accident, Maurya had assigned Amir to a near full time protection of his little sister. In many ways, Amir was the perfect foil for her. They both regaled in each other's silence. While others kept trying to cajole conversations out of Maya, Amir let her be.

He had begun to see in her the sister that he had lost. As long as no words were exchanged, he could pretend that it was the same girl, and he could do now what he had failed to do then – protect her with his life. Amir's world view had been broken almost irreparably by the trauma of his childhood. But now, for the first time in his life, he was beginning to develop two new feelings – loyalty towards Maurya and an inexplicable affection towards Maya.

She'd paint in the garden, and he'd sit close by; she'd catch him looking, but she never found it disturbing. Perhaps because she had found in those eyes what everyone had missed, a lonely kindness. It is possible that they managed to connect because he saw the same in her eyes.

"What is it that you are painting?" he asked her.

"Just stuff," she answered. "I'm trying to practice a style called Cubism. I'm using cubes and other geometrical shapes to try and abstract all possible viewpoints of this person."

He kept looking at the painting for a few minutes, and then said, "it reminds me of Maurya."

Maya had been scared at the interpretation that she had thought was only obvious to her, and yet he had seen right through it. Was she so transparent? She decided to test her painting with the cook, and when he didn't have a similar interpretation, her fear gave in to curiosity.

"Why are you just sitting there and watching?" she asked Amir one day, "would you like to paint?"

"I don't know how."

"I can teach you."

"I've never been taught anything. I'm not sure if I'm capable of learning."

She had laughed, "Of course, you are. We all are."

He hadn't realised it in the beginning, but throwing those colours on canvas would go on to become his salvation in life. Maya would teach Amir little by little, and he soon forgot about his past and present, and focused instead on bringing to life an image in his mind down to the canvas.

A lot of what he drew had tinges of sadness. It was so much easier to understand than any other feeling for Amir. Not every person in the world may know happiness intimately, but there is a measure of sadness alive in everyone. He had found that the thing he really needed to do was to embrace it. He did not seek for it to consume him – no, nope, nada. He needed it to add sense to the chaos inside him, the funnel to his emotions, the pathway to hitherto unvoiced ideas – he needed to embrace his sadness in its vast extreme, where it become the same as joy. For indeed in its true primal form, he had found that there is no difference between the way the two feel. It was not to be hated. It was to be acknowledged.

Without realising, this form of digression began to give him peace. He painted with his heart and in turn the paintings managed to tell him that not much had been in his control then. That was when he decided to break a promise to his mother and travel back to his village.

The visit would end up being a short one. Both of them were so long gone that only vague memories remained in people's mind, and then too the memories were inconsistent, as if different people remembered different mothers which eventually coalesced into who they believed to be the same person.

Amir painted more and more with Maya when he got back to the city and he finally realised that while he would never be able to forgive himself completely, he had managed to isolate the poisonous part of himself in colour and put it down to paper just so that all other parts of him could go on living.

Maurya walked in on one of their sessions one afternoon. "Boy, your mother should have named you Picasso." Amir couldn't help but smile at that, and the three of them stood there in the garden in a brief surreal moment connecting them, lost in the rare smile of a man they had all thought, himself including, to be beyond redemption. "I never knew such talent resided in our little family," he said.

The magnitude of Maurya using the word 'family' was neither accidental, nor would it go unnoticed by the other two. For a moment, Maya forgot her improper love, and Amir felt a warmth that comes with the knowledge of trust and belonging.

***

During the day, Maya would digress whichever way was possible, to not think about Maurya. At night she would lie awake staring at the ceiling. They tried to continue their weekly dinners, but she slowly shied away from activities such as movies or games that might put them alone in each other's company for an extended period of time.

"Maya?" he called out to her from the kitchen on a day when the servants were out. Maurya had given them the day off, "I'm cooking tonight."

"Why can't we order something?"

"Because then you'll quickly wolf down your food and run back into hiding," he said. "This way we'll get to spend at least a couple of hours with each other."

This scared her, he gave her a reassuring smile.

"That is quite unnecessary, you know."

"Au contraire, mon... ma... sœur," his struggle with words made her smile. Then she regretted it immediately afterward because it gave him the confidence to continue on with his plans for the evening.

"I can't find the strainer," he said. "Do you know where the cook keeps it?" he asked.

"I think it's in the cabinet behind you." She looked on as he struggled with the pots.

She looked on nervously and then moved forward impatiently. She edged past him and reached into the cabinet to pull out the strainer. The downside of the movement was that when she turned around, she had inadvertently snuggled right up to Maurya. She pushed a hand through her hair nervously, twice. Three times would have been too many, so she pulled her other hand that held the strainer and put it between them.

He smiled and took it gently out of her hand, oblivious to her discomfort.

"Are you old enough to have a beer?" he asked her as he moved back towards the soup.

"I don't know, how old do you have to be?"

"I guess what I was asking was if you'd had alcohol before with your friends."

"No."

"Well, what the heck," he pulled out a couple of bottles and passed one over to her, "you are almost eighteen now. Just don't tell Vishnu."

He laughed as she sniffed it and then took her first sip. She had scrunched up her nose and gagged. "You'll get used to it," he said to her.

"Why would I want to get used to it?" she asked.

He laughed, "You'll either like how it tastes or how it makes you feel. Maybe both."

"I'll have to take your word for it."

Joking about alcohol had managed to shift focus away from her feelings to something more trivial. She appreciated that Maurya had sensed her tenseness and tried to ease that, but that only served to remind her of how she truly felt about him, which brought her back to the proverbial square one.

They managed to joke about things. He told her stories of him struggling through the early days of Father's influence on his career and how even though the times had been cruel, the one good thing to come out of it was that she had been spared.

"Times haven't been that cruel, you know," she finally said.

"What do you mean?"

"We went through things that everyone has to go through in life. Loss of your loved ones is an unfortunate certainty. In our case, these events occurred far sooner than we'd have hoped for. But it is a matter of probability, and it's not necessarily times' fault. At an average through our life, time would give us as many boring moments as anyone else."

He nodded thoughtfully, "I see that you've been reading Seneca."

He gave her a hug at the end of the evening, and she timidly put her arms around him in response. Later, as she lay in bed, she thought that things might simplify after all. She had felt peace when he hugged her. The feeling was short lived and soon she was tossing and turning replaying the events of the evening in her head. The hug had been a mistake, now she had a memory of his arms around her. The cocktail of emotions was beginning to overpower her as a fire threatened to consume her body. She reached between her legs with a hand to quell it.

She felt an insane urge to see him and crept out of her room to his. He was talking on the phone; she gently eased the door open ever so slowly to peek inside just as she heard a woman's voice come through. He wasn't alone in the room. The conversation stopped as she stumbled, the door jumped an inch or two and Maurya stepped up to open it.

"I'm sorry," Maya said. "I should have knocked, but I didn't know that you have company." She took a step backward as the woman swung into view, "I just wanted to thank you for tonight."

She turned around before he could respond and crept back into bed, hoping that the darkness would swallow her forever.

***

As things eased up, Amir was slowly eased back to be close to Maurya again. He observed from the side-lines as Maurya, and Vishnu quietly extended their regional influence and slowly pulled at the support that had been earlier directed towards Dhanraj Nanda.

Amir's men also managed to coax Dhanraj's workers into a strike, bringing the company to a standstill. The strike was a particular masterstroke, but it required some financial coaxing accompanied by an adequate amount of force. Over the years, Dhanraj had hardly endeared himself to his workers who were none too shy to be able to make an easy extra buck, and yet some workers tried to get into a more prominent share of the pie and refused to back down. Amir suppressed such oppressions swiftly with the adequate amount of force. Five bullets shut down five thousand dissenters and even though the other side shot some bullets of their own, Amir clinically hunted down and eliminated potential risks. The days where Maurya operated in silence behind his ring of protection were gone. He now had the financial clout to employ an army that outnumbered his enemy's.

Maurya and Vishnu were routinely summoned back to Nanda's office who was trying to cling to any semblance of control that he could muster. On each occasion, they politely apologised for transgressions and promised to take rectifying measures. Every meeting was followed by some weeks of calmness and a subsequent storm. Amir would usually be present at these meetings to observe, and he saw the arrogant aristocrat being reduced to a glowering frail old man in less than five years.

A lot of Maurya and Vishnu's discussions would occur in the car with him present and that was usually enough to keep him appraised of the progress.

Maurya didn't smoke and drank alcohol extremely infrequently. There were no lavish parties at the house even though frequent dinners were arranged to socialise with friends, acquaintances and the occasional enemy that had to be kept close. Maya, who was turning nineteen now, had stepped into the role of the lady of the household.

It was one such evening close to the end, when Dhanraj and Amita had been invited for a party, along with some other cartel members. Over the past couple of years, Maurya had become an increasingly prominent player in the circles. Word had reached him that the government was planning on opening a bid for a set of trans-national highways and he had invited the members from the west and the east to outline strategies. The meeting was a slap in the face for Dhanraj because it should have been him calling out to the cartel to request their presence. But not only had Maurya bypassed him to take that honour, the cartel's response had indicated that they too were beginning to see him as their representative in the north.

Towards the end of the evening, Amita had accosted Maurya angrily, most likely in defiance for the disrespect towards her husband. Maurya had quietly grasped her elbow and led her into the kitchen. Amir followed behind quietly to make sure that his boss was okay, though it was hardly likely that Dhanraj would try to hurt Maurya in his own house, with members of the cartel present.

The two of them were alone in the kitchen and terse words were being exchanged. As he watched, Maurya reached out with a calming hand and put it on her cheek, then slowly reached forward and planted a kiss on her lips. There was a familiarity in the kiss that surprised Amir. He suspected that them coming together might have happened at the time that he had been busy protecting Maya.

As he watched, the urgency of Amita's embrace grew; they broke apart for a few seconds during which Maurya looked up at Amir. He gave him a short near imperceptible nod and Amir turned around and walked back to the entrance of the kitchen. The sounds and shuffles from inside indicated that the activities inside had grown more heated. Maurya never ceased to surprise Amir, but fucking Dhanraj's wife while he was in the next room was boldness bordering on insanity.

A few minutes later Dhanraj walked over to Amir. "Have you seen my wife?" he asked gruffly with a disdain that the rich folk usually reserved for people they thought were beneath them, "we need to leave."

Amir nodded, "I think I saw her go past this door some time ago," he said even as Amita's soft moans reached him.

Amir watched the old man move past him into the kitchen and stop short only a few steps inside. His body stiffened as he looked as his young adversary engaged in coitus with his wife. To his credit, Dhanraj's stiff bearing faltered only ever so slightly as he turned around and walked past Amir, "I guess I can wait a while more."

His outward assurance began to fade as he hurried to put some distance between himself and the kitchen door and he stumbled over a vase which crashed to the ground. He brushed off the looks from the people as he picked himself up and walked towards the bar.

Amir was not a person who took pleasure in other people's pain, but he could hardly contain the satisfaction that came from watching Dhanraj's defeated form withdraw from the scene.

"Why isn't anyone cleaning the mess?" Maya had snuck up on him while his eyes had been on the old man. She turned around and walked past him into the kitchen before he could stop her.

Book V

29
Caesar

Zurich
August, 2015

There are three stages to dying, I've come to understand. First, it takes a few moments to get over the shock of the knowledge that it had managed to creep up on you unknowingly, and that the invincibility of youth which had slowly waned had hit an abrupt end in the moment that was now. But once you are over that, the second thing you might do is to try and live, for it was really either that or curling up and waiting for the end – which was also incidentally the third stage, preceded by a smaller half a stage of resignation.

Caesar had to try and live now.

"I need to speak to the manager about the service here." The men duly continued to ignore him.

The last three hours had been a blur. Caesar had been driven to a villa instead of his hotel. Fitful sleep had wrapped most of his journey. From what he could make out, they had gone past the city and driven along the Zürichsee for about twenty minutes before turning away from the lake.

They had driven to the back of a building and then led him straight up to the top floor, where three fairly large men greeted him with looks of profound displeasure.

Caesar jumped in surprise on spotting Mishka there before realising a moment later that the man's appearance was slightly off. He had a thinner jaw, ears that looked fine on Mishka were too large on his narrower face. The words he whispered in Caesar's ears as he punched him in the gut brought the much-needed clarification, "You killed my brother."

"Beg your pardon?" Caesar asked between gasps, but instead of an answer, a crack to his back followed.

"We had an accident," he continued, nonetheless. "I did not kill him. A car hit us, and I climbed out and escaped."

Mishka's twin continued hitting him.

"I figured if I stayed there the police would come, and then there would be more trouble. I did warn the big brute to be careful about his little spins."

The blows didn't stop and soon Caesar was curled up on the floor. One of the other men in the room decided that the spectacle was getting boring and joined in on hitting their captive.

"What, did you think that the Russian wasn't doing justice to the job of beating me up?"

He must have passed out because the next time he blinked his eyes open, it was dark outside.

"Life is tough, eh?" he gritted through his lips that were covered with dried blood as they picked him up and started hauling him out of the room.

He tried to flex his toes, but they didn't respond to his mental probes.

"C'est la *fucking* vie," he whispered again, but the men showed no inclination to reply.

A few minutes later, he was propped up on a dining table. The Don sat on the other side digging into a steak with relish. He looked up for a minute as they set Caesar down and then went back to his food.

"You have a lovely place here," Caesar looked at the eating man. "Have I taken the opportunity to thank you for your hospitality? Though if I may venture a bit of constructive criticism, these men could use some lessons in public discourse."

The man in front of him continued eating.

"I see that you are enjoying a delectable Valpolicella. Though after the day I've had, you can hardly fault me for desiring a stiff whisky to calm those nerves."

The Don's shrug was too subtle for Caesar to notice. But the Russian behind him must have registered it because a minute later his fist slammed into Caesar's neck pushing his face violently forward into the table. The nose smarted and the neck screamed, but the silver lining was that he was beginning to sense his toes again.

"I see that this isn't quite the place where criticism is taken well. If I may, my friend – this attitude may come in the way of development as you move further along the career ladder. Unless of course your job requirements strictly need you to be a dumb asshole, in which case I think your future potential is exemplary."

The Russian stepped forward to hit him again.

"Wait!" Caesar held a hand up when he saw the Don was unlikely to intervene. "What's your name, Mishka's brother?"

The man stopped at the question, was that all it took to engage him? As if he hadn't been trying to do that for the past three hours.

"Evgeni."

"Evgeni," he repeated. "Listen Jenia? Can I call you Jenia?" I continued without waiting for an answer. "I'm sorry that your brother died, and I promise that I would have done anything in my power to prevent his death if I could."

"Enough!" the Don's words boomed out from across the table as a server took the last of his meal away. "You are quite the talker Signor Caesar, but the time for talking is done. You've cost me a hundred million euros and a faithful irreplaceable man."

"Seriously, irreplaceable?" Caesar looked towards Evgeni. "You have a near exact replica standing less than six feet away."

"Quiet!" the Don's raised hand leapt to his rescue as if to strengthen his need for silence. "We need to finish the transaction." He nodded at the men standing behind Caesar, one of whom stepped forward with Caesar's old suitcase and dumped it on the table in front of him.

"We took the liberty of checking you out of the hotel."

"You needn't have taken the trouble."

"Nonetheless, we did. Do whatever it takes. We have thirty minutes on the clock before we kill Octavia. Another half hour after that before we kill you."

Caesar's throat was beginning to dry. Perhaps it was the exertion his body had gone through, but it could also have been because of the dried blood in his mouth. The next words he spoke came out like a croak. "But you see that you have managed to put us in a particularly difficult situation." The Don raised his eyebrows, and the gambler continued, "The moment I hand over the money to you, both my fate and Octavia's is completely in your hands. In which scenario, considering your penchant for violence, you are very likely to kill us both, thus making it an unattractive alternative for me.

"Now you do realise that the only connection you have between the money and you is me, which implies that if you decide to kill me, you lose access to the money as well, which not only makes that scenario bad for both of us, it also makes your threat *incredible*. Given a choice between giving you the money and taking away your incentive to keep me alive, against not giving you the money and preserving the incentive, you know what the smart choice is bound to be.

"Knowing that you have an incentive to keep me alive, and that I have an incentive to not give you the money, the decision for killing Octavia becomes pointless. You are a smart man, and I don't think you'll indulge in pointless murders. If you want any more proof about the futility of this, let me tell you this – kill her or let her go. I don't care. Not while my own life is bound to a sinking rock.

"Which brings us down to this. I have the following choices – either give up the money to you out of the kindness of my heart and the fear of pain, or to give in to the pain and wait for the slow death that is sure to follow. You see we do not have an equilibrium here since our choices are contradictory. How do you propose that we resolve this?"

The silence weighed down upon the room. Then the Don gestured to Jenia who came forward and slammed his fist to the back of his head, which bounced forward and hit the table again.

"You do have an ability to put many words together and make surprisingly little sense," the Don said as his head rang from the dual blow.

"Little sense, man, have you never studied game theory?"

The Don did not respond immediately. A few thoughtful minutes later he looked up. "You speak too much, old Caesar, and I'm tired of your games. I will have the money back, no questions. As for your life, I'm willing to play you for it."

"Play for it?"

"I'll give you one last chance to meet me at the poker table. Closed game. Before we start, you transfer the money to my account and after that, we play for your freedom. If you lose, we take your life for Mishka's; if you win, we let you walk away."

"And what's stopping ol' Jenia from driving over me with a truck the moment I step out?"

"We'll bring an interloper to run the game. You can even suggest one if you want. If you win, we will continue to stay in the room without any outside communication while the casino drops you off at the airport. You are free to charter a flight to wherever you want. You'd have to agree that once you are far away and I have the money, there is no incentive for me to chase after you."

Another day to live. Caesar said, "If it is not too much trouble for you, can I have that whisky while I think about it?"

The Don nodded, and a man stepped forward, almost too soon, as if he'd been waiting in the shadows with a bottle in hand. "One more thing," Caesar said as they poured him a drink. "You will let the girl go free, right?"

The Don gave him an appraising look. "I thought you did not care for her?"

"I don't," he answered. "Not a lot in the very least, but it'll be good to know that I do not have the blood of another human being on my hands."

The Don glanced behind Caesar at Jenia. "You did kill one of my men; there should be an apt payment for it."

"I thought the hundred million was an apt payment for it. And you have put my own life on a game."

"Very well," the Don nodded towards one of his men. "Call the men and let her go, have them leave her near a hospital." He turned his attention back towards Caesar. "Yourself though, this is the final deal we'll make. Any other deviations and I'll swallow the loss and kill you."

Caesar nodded. He let the coldness inside the pit of his stomach swell outwards into his heart and then allowed it to sneak into his words, "You see Don, you can't really kill a dead man; you can only set him free."

Another day to live. *Another day to cheat.* Another day to die.

30
Caesar

Zurich
August, 2015

"Can you repeat the terms of the transactions today?" the interloper asked. They were sitting in a private room in the basement of the casino.

The Don looked at Caesar as he spoke. "We will play for this man's freedom today. If he wins, the casino will transfer him to a private location known only to him and the casino. If, on the other hand, he loses, my men will take him away and act as we deem appropriate."

The interloper slowly wrote everything down on a paper, then looked up at Caesar when he had finished, "Do you agree to this?" The fact that no legal tender would approve of the document wasn't enough to perturb the interloper. What we agreed on was sanctimonious, something that no man in the room would consider reneging on.

"I agree," the heavy words escaped Caesar's lips.

"Then let the terms of the transaction be final. Are there any final actions that we should commit to before we start?"

"There is a matter of a personal transaction that we'll need to close before we begin. Mr Caesar is aware of it."

A man standing at the back of the room brought Caesar his case, from which he removed the laptop and the device he needed to complete the transfer.

"I would like to make a bank transfer for a hundred million euros," he said when a banker picked up the phone on the second ring.

"Certainly, can you please key in the account number in the application that is open on your laptop?" Neither the nature of the call nor the size of the transaction seemed to surprise the man on the other end.

Caesar entered the number without comment. The banker responded as the information reached him, "Thank you. This is the private account listed under the name of a Mr F. A. Could you please confirm your identity by entering your personal password on the device?"

The phone was on the speaker so that the others could hear the conversation. Seven pairs of eyes looked at Caesar as he keyed in the numbers. "Thank you. We will now do a voice recognition check, can you say the phrase – 'Leave the gun, take the Cannoli?

Caesar repeated the words while the others looked on.

"Thank you, sir. Can you please enter the account number for the recipient in the application." Caesar looked down at the paper slip that he had been given by the Don's entourage and typed in a number, "I have initiated the transfer," the banker finally said. "The transaction should be completed within the next hour."

All that the room could muster was silence as he ended the call. The last seventy-two hours weighed heavily on everyone. Well... everyone but the interloper who had no idea of what was happening.

"Call the bank," the Don finally said.

"May I have some whisky?" Caesar broke the silence that followed by addressing the interloper.

"Are you sure you want to drink before the game?" he asked.

"Very sure."

"You understand that it may affect your clarity of thought?"

"Yes, kind sir. I thank you for your concern for my cognizance. But if it blurs out that Russian's ugly face, I'd consider it a well-balanced risk."

Jenia shuffled in his place as if gunning to get a shot at his face again. But this was a place where verbal assaults were allowed far more readily than physical ones.

The room reverted back to its state of a temporary uneasy stupor as Caesar sipped his whisky and the others looked at him with stony faces. About ten minutes had passed when the man the Don had sent out returned and whispered in the old man's ears.

"It seems that you have finally done something according to plan and saved us some trouble. Now we can move to the second part of the transaction. I'd have you know that I do not like unnecessary violence. But I will play this game for the loyal man I lost because of you."

Caesar nodded and raised the glass. He looked directly at Evgeni, "To Mishka."

31
Caesar

Zurich
August, 2015

We began with a million euros in chips. The chips had no value beyond the game, apart from the life they represented. We would play till both the hands on the clock touched twelve, or till one of us lost all his chips to the other.

"Pair beats high card." I lost a little.

Where could I go? In the discussions, we had managed to overlook the painstakingly gathered two million euros of mine that I had brought into the game three days ago, or the money I'd won from our other friends. As far as he was concerned, he had begun to look at it all as if it was his cash. For all intents and purposes, I suppose it was now.

"Straight beats three of a kind." I lost some more.

Was I worried? Yes. I'd put my life on the line many times before, but I'd never risked losing it. All those times, the biggest risk had been of my cash balances hitting reset. There was no reset after this if this went south.

"Flush beats straight." I lost some more.

No game moves in one direction all the time.

"Four of a kind beats full house." I lost some more.

This game had progressed unusually.

"Royal flush beats straight flush." Was it me imagining it or was the interloper blushing in embarrassment as the truth of the situation finally dawned on me? This was never meant to be a contest.

The Don sat back contentedly as Jenia grabbed me by the shoulder and whisked me away.

"Where are you taking me, Evgeni?" I asked them as we drove away from the casino, "Back to the house?"

The Russian sat with another man in the front seat. They handcuffed and thrust me in the back seat of a Peugeot.

"No, we don't go back to the house. Boss didn't want you getting his house dirty."

"Ha," a wry laugh escaped me unasked, "What are you going to do with me then?"

The Russian had the courtesy to turn back and look me in the eye as he answered, "We take you to the middle of Zurichsee in a boat, then shoot you, tie your body to a rock and dump you in the lake."

"That sounds just terrible," I said. "Anyway, what do I care? If I am, death is not, if death is, I am not. Have you heard of Epicurus? Smart bloke, you must read him sometime." I looked out of the window as the memory of an earlier evening floated past me, "I do hope that the rope breaks and then I float up and freak out some stupid tourists, fucking millennials and their travel crap. Speaking of, do you have any fucking alcohol on you?"

The Russian leaned forward after a few seconds and dished out a small bottle of liquor from the glove compartment, which I took happily.

"What is wrong with this?" I said as I took a sip of the disgusting fluid.

"It is Unicum. It is from Hungary, very herbal."

"Great, I can't believe that the last thing I'll drink before I die is this fucking herbal alcohol." It was time for a last play. "I had a Romanian friend who told me a joke about Hungary, do you want to hear it?"

The men in the front grunted in response. "How did you sink a Hungarian battleship?"

"How?" The Russian asked after a moment.

"You put it in the water." I waited for the laughter to follow but none came.

"I don't understand," Jenia finally said.

"Forget it, do you know any Russian jokes?"

"Yes," he said.

"Tell me," Anything to keep me from thinking about what was coming.

"Knock knock," Jenia complied.

"Who's there?"

"I'm going to shoot you in your face tonight," he answered. "Now shut up and sit quietly, stupid gambler with stupid jokes."

The way he said it reminded me of Mishka. I couldn't help but feel a tinge of sadness, but then Mishka probably had it coming for him at some point of time.

Boy had already given me up for dead. I had been so close to escaping this all, ending this journey and starting another chapter. I didn't have many regrets apart from the one. The last game, that was always going to be my bane wasn't it. In a way, it was fitting that it should end over a game of poker. *Glamorous*. I had squeezed all the juice out of all the lemons I had, that had kept me from puking my guts out for the most part but now was the time to let lose all the gut of misfortune that I'd trapped inside myself.

We finally stopped at a small private dock, and I was transferred onto a boat.

"May I tell you a short story, Jenia? Would you humour me?" I asked him.

He grunted again.

"There was a girl I loved once, but I had to run away from her because I was changing, and I didn't want her to see that

I was. I thought at that time that it would break her heart. "

The boat's gentle purr echoed mildly around us.

She said she felt betrayed. But she also said that she felt she was losing her battle. That her answers were no longer the same and that she needed my help to find new ones. You know what she did eventually, Jenia? She tried to hurt me and when she failed, she tried to hurt herself. I thought it was a mighty stupid thing to do, Jenia. What do you think? But you see, the day it happened, something within me ceased to exist. There are no loose ends now, no further dots to connect. After you kill me tonight, there is no one to take this story forward."

They stopped the boat and the man with the hat started wrapping a thick chain around my feet before passing it through a loop and shackling the two ends to a large stone.

"Surely you don't believe that this is going to hold forever?" I was speaking mechanically by now.

"It'll hold for the right amount of time," the man by my feet said. There may have been something familiar about that voice, but I had reached a point where voices and sight merged together into an immense blob of meaningless nothingness.

"Goodbye," Jenia said and took his gun out, but his companion stopped him.

"Remember the orders," the man said. "I get to shoot him."

Jenia reluctantly moved aside.

The man stepped forward and finally raised his head so I could see his face.

Maurya's face was the last thing I saw as the muffled sound of the bullets broke the silence. His eyes bore into mine as he reached out and pushed me over the edge into the icy water as a final deliverance.

This is how it ends.

Interlude

I
Maurya

Zurich
August, 2015

My name is Maurya, we've met a short while before. Life has taught me; that is both a long and short span of time. A long time to live, a short time to bear a grudge.

What is a man? A sum of his actions? Or a product of his circumstances? Modern psychology says that the most of who you are as a person is developed and set by the time one ends adolescence. Does that mean that a man is a stable entity beyond a certain age? Hardly, would be my first response, but let's take a quick step back before we dive too deep into this.

"This is a rather unusual request, Maurya," Don Camorra frowned at me across the table.

I couldn't help but smile, "I understand that, Don. I have a score to settle, surely you understand the importance of satisfying one's debts."

I left it at that.

"I have a lot of respect for you, and it is for this that I shall grant this request," the Don said. "But I have two things for you to note. One, when the time comes for me to remind you of this, you will respond within reason without question." The Don was good at letting the important things unsaid and yet the person on the other end could not feign ignorance. “Two, should anything surprising happen during the event, it is unlikely to go down well for anyone involved. We will all lose, and you know well that I despise losing.”

“I understand fully. I appreciate the accommodation you are making for me,” I said to the Don. “A debt needs to be repaid, and in return, I take on the debt of your words.”

II
August

Victoria
August, 2016

What thinks a man, as he sinks to his death,
the thrashing body, the flailing mind,
sinking under the weight of stones that bind,
that mattered not that I'll no longer live,
does matter that what I leave behind?
That it does but, does it that?

I know barely who I was, I see faces not,
For I am now a sinking man,
and a sinking man thinks not,
but thrashes and flails
towards the hand
that shall save him, or that shall take him across.

The weight of life, finally gone,
Why choose to live like I did?
Burning, chasing, desires, glory
Love and hate, and the end of story

The one thing that hurts the most,
Is the answer I couldn't find,
The question that knew me best
The question I leave behind.

III
Don Camorra

Campania
August, 2015

"What did the bank say?" the Don asked.

"Our bank received a notification for the transaction at 18:06 from Caesar's bank. The notification indicated that a hundred million euros had been sanctioned for transfer to our account. But the transaction failed because of a filing error on the part of Caesar's bank."

It had been three days since the last game. He was back in his villa in Lecce near the southern parts of Italia. They were standing in a large hallway. The Don was looking at a large canvas. An angel hung in the air with a scroll dangling from his hands with the words *Gloria in Eccelsis Deo* written from it. It pointed at the sky, as if reassuring baby Jesus that he was indeed the son of God, while the Archdeacon Lawrence and St Francis looked over the virgin and her new-born.

"What does that mean?"

The man hesitated for a few seconds. "The bank says that it was a system error, and they need Caesar to sanction the transaction again, but..."

The Don turned around to look at his messenger. "Go on."

"We fear that Caesar may have bungled the transaction deliberately, forcing the bank into logging an incorrect transfer request, which would mean..."

"That he fooled us."

"That is likely, Don."

The Don turned around and began walking towards his study, leaving the majestic Caravaggio behind. The messenger followed behind him. "We still have Caesar's things, and we tried to recreate the transaction following up from how we saw him do it, but..."

"The money is gone," said the Don with an air of finality.

"Yes, sir," he finally conceded.

Don Camorra's eyes were cold steel. "At least he died for it."

IV
Maurya and all his unfortunate friends

India
1985 - 2000

As the British empire professionalised the administration in the country, the old aristocratic families found themselves pushed out of a job. A lot of these families fell away into a slow ruin, but as the country devolved into chaos around the time that British were thinking of leaving, the more opportunistic families staked claim to large swathes of land. After independence, this physical asset would prove crucial as a form of trade for wealth and influence and help them re-establish a new form of control. As the first few decades turned, these rich heirs formed a club of sorts, working heavily on system of providing mutual hand jobs to get off.

The new elite that had emerged from the old guard in the four decades since Nehru raised the flag proved to be even more territorial than their forefathers. These people had come close to losing all their wealth and would go to any lengths to prevent it from occurring again.

As the only son and first offspring born into the household after the country became independent, Dhanraj had been given a free rein, which he had exploited to the fullest. After spending the first forty years of his life taking his pick of the local women, wine and food, he was close to satiated on life and his family finally broached the subject of procuring a further offspring to take the family name down to the next generation. Quite fortuitously, his manager had a perfect match in mind and introduced his own twenty-three-year-old daughter to Dhanraj. While at other times the family might have objected to the age gap between Dhanraj and his wife to be, they were happy to live with it, as long as Dhanraj himself was willing to give up his bachelorhood.

The wedding was rapidly executed and Dhanraj and his young wife set about to fulfil the grandparent's expectations of rapidly bringing a few grandkids into the world. Alas, but it wasn't to be. Seven years would pass without the conception of a child and the family decided that perhaps another prospective mother needed to be found. Dhanraj's manager and father-in-law, who had tied his own fortunes after retirement to the connection of his bloodline to the Nanda family, rolled the dice by putting forward the name of his younger daughter, the now twenty-year-old Amita as a prospective second bride for Dhanraj.

The family had shown some scepticism towards bringing in another daughter from the same family into their home. After all, the first one had not proven to be quite as fertile as they had hoped, not to mention the age gap between Dhanraj and their new prospective daughter-in-law, which would swell to twenty-seven years. By now Dhanraj had turned a sprightly old forty-seven and his interest in children had waned before it could pick up much momentum. Needless to say he didn't care much for a second marriage, but over the years, he had developed a strong crush on Amita. A low-key ceremony was arranged, at the end of which, the older sister was sent to live in a farmhouse in the hills while Amita moved into the house in her sister's place.

She wasn't unhappy at how it all played out, even though this was far from how she had imagined her future unfolding. She had spent the last decade or so thinking of a handsome swashbuckling young husband who could last longer than the ceremonial seven minutes in bed. She had also dreamt of finishing her education to become a lawyer. Amita was as smart as she was pretty. As a first act, she sat down and negotiated a return to university with her husband; in the second act she fucked him silly.

She put Dhanraj on a relatively rigid schedule that allowed him to drink alcohol only twice a week, combined with a low cholesterol vegetarian diet and five kilometres a day on the jogger.

Amita felt that she had done her bit for the family. She had married a man more than twice her age for the sake of securing financial stability for them all. She had even managed to establish a level of camaraderie with her husband. All of this had destroyed her relationship with her sister, but she couldn't find a way to blame herself for it.

Amita was a woman of high intelligence, who had apparently taken the old adage of 'work hard party harder' to heart. If she had to imagine a movie star *or two* while she made love to her husband – she was happy doing it as long as it got the job done.

"Which one of us is better in bed?" she had jokingly asked Dhanraj once.

"Between you or your sister?" he asked.

"Yeah?"

"I cannot say," the man who had slept with over a hundred women in his life had become embarrassed at the prospect of talking about sex.

One time after he had come home from a visit to his regular escort, she had adamantly demanded that he procure a male prostitute for her so that she could partake too.

"Women in our house don't do that."

"Well, they should." She left it at that as a warning.

She went back to university and for good measure managed to persuade her husband to sponsor her in setting up an environmental law practice. Unfortunately, or fortunately, five more years of pleasure and pain would produce no children. The family tried to raise the prospect of a third marriage, but by now, both Dhanraj and his father were tiring of the cycle. Moreover, all said and done, Dhanraj was quite smitten with his wife and could not harbour the thought of parting from her.

Nanda senior passed on a couple of years later, and the topic of grandkids was put to rest.

It was around this time that Amita met Maurya for the first time at their farmhouse. He was an earnest young lad, around the same age as her. She felt a twinge of guilt as her husband gloated about running him out of business that evening.

But, Maurya and Vishnu looked like they came from money and would have something to work with. They were undoubtedly starting from a position of far greater comfort than most people who dared to dream. Far below the glass ceiling, there is another ceiling for people like Amita. She liked to think of it as a barrier made from poisonous asbestos. This was the barrier of poverty, education, and influence. Amita had done what she had to do to break through.

She imagined she was with Maurya when she slept with Dhanraj that night, and once a serviceable orgasm had been achieved, put him out of her mind completely. He wouldn't come up again until a few months later when an angry Dhanraj had cursed them over dinner. It appeared as if they were managing to stir up a little more trouble than Dhanraj had earlier anticipated.

During this time, environmental issues weren't receiving the sense of urgency that she felt they deserved – she had managed to set up a small office with a few employees, but the funding emerged mostly from her husband's commercial projects. As Dhanraj's anxiety towards his business grew, his liquid position declined. Before long, it had begun to have an impact on Amita's practice. She was about to let go of her first employees, citing her inability to pay their salaries, when Maurya dropped by her office with a sizable donation.

"Whatever is happening between me, and your husband should not come in the way of your good work," he said.

"But I cannot accept this, out of principle and loyalty to my husband," she replied.

"That is for you to decide," he said, "how does your work and your identity stand against your loyalty towards your husband... and your sister?" He had let the last words hang.

"Why are we fighting here, Dhanraj?" She asked her husband that night, "Can't we just retire to Switzerland or something? You've had your fun and your heart isn't quite in it. Let these guys play."

"And make me a joke in front of the cartel? Enough is enough. I'm going to get them killed."

"Is that really necessary?"

"We need to send a message."

"Maybe you only need to get one of them killed then."

He pondered at her comment, "That might be right. Which one?"

"The old one seems to be the brains." She said, plus she couldn't imagine Maurya's pretty face to be disfigured by bullets and stuff.

It turned out that Vishnu and Maurya were significantly better protected than Dhanraj had hoped.

He sent a few men after Maurya's sister, but that failed as well.

They met again at a cartel dinner where a few pleasantries were exchanged. It was there that Maurya proposed they have dinner to speak about her projects. She acquiesced because it seemed harmless.

One dinner turned into another, and before she knew it, she was spending an evening at one of his apartments in outer Delhi. Even though she had imagined this happening hundreds of times before, cheating on her husband filled her with a little regret.

They both thought of it as sex between two friends and work associates, a singularly personal aspect to a strictly professional relationship otherwise. But once the veil of lust subsided, she began to see the devotion and sincerity in Maurya's eyes. He was thoughtful in ways that other men in her life hadn't been. While Dhanraj had only afforded her a grudging respect, Maurya never needed to be reminded of her status as an equal in their partnership.

"I'm going to have to destroy your husband."

"Now, is *that* really necessary?"

"Yes."

"It is between you two. Do not involve me."

"I cannot promise that, unfortunately. Tell me what he values the most in the world?"

She laughed a mirthless laugh, "His pride."

"Cometh before a fall," he said. "He needs to see me having sex with you."

"Really, is that all you can think of doing to hurt his pride? Fuck 'his woman'. You men, for all of your intelligence and ambition, can be quite stupid."

The event at the party at his house had followed. Soon after which Dhanraj's health declined rapidly. Following the pretext of a household argument, she had consigned herself to sleeping in the guest bedroom.

"Is it because you can't get your fill of fucking your boyfriend?" He had spat at her, and at that point, the need for all pretexts had vanished. In the months that followed, Maurya would arrive at their farmhouse late in the evenings. On one occasion, Dhanraj had come into her room after

Maurya had left and had sex with her as if to exert a minute semblance of control.

"I'm sorry Dhanraj," she had said as they lay there afterwards. "I'm not doing this to spite you. I do love him."

"I've been nothing but kind towards you," he said.

"I'm sure you believe that," she had said.

This had spelled the end of their relationship, and he quietly passed on a year later. Maurya and Amita waited for a few months and then formalised their relationship with marriage.

Amita, assuming the role of the lady of the household, had the unintended effect of Maya slowly getting pushed out of the role.

Not wanting to resort to half measures, the younger woman chose to move out altogether. "I want to study art," Maya said to Maurya one evening not long after.

"Of course, do you have a school in mind?"

"Les Beaux-arts de Paris."

"So far away, but we've only just got back together."

"I know, but you have Amita in your life now. You don't really need me around."

Fear had sprung up on Maurya's face on the realisation that along the way, he had failed in some way to stay connected to her. "That's not true at all," he said earnestly. "You both have a different but equally important place in my life."

Maya grew quiet for a while. "I want to go, it is but one life, after all."

Maurya gave in without further fight.

"It shall be done," he said. "I'd presume that it's a prestigious institution, we need to work towards getting you prepared."

"I have already started, my language tutor will start tomorrow, we will study four days a week. My contemporary arts teacher would start spending eight hours with me on the other three days. I'll have some hours of philosophy tutoring every week which should help me find my, for the lack of a better word, *voice*."

"I'm impressed; how long do you see yourself working through this schedule?"

"I hope to apply in a year and half's time," she said. "I'll be out of your way in less than two years."

"What if I don't want you out of my way?"

She shrugged. "It shall happen nevertheless."

While Maya planned her temporary departure, Vishnu threw another little curve ball towards Maurya by expressing an interest to retire. "Not right away, but we need to start grooming my successor."

"That is impossible to find," Maurya had despaired. "I need a confidant here that I could trust with my life."

"Haven't you already found the person?"

Vishnu expressed his vision to groom Amita to take his place. The difficult part was convincing her to give up on her law practice.

Maurya's new digression was to build hotels. A few years ago, Maurya had been contacted by Mahesh, the son of the cartel member from the West. Mahesh had opened to him with his vision to build a luxury hotel on the west coast. His business plan had failed to evoke enough enthusiasm in his own father, who had doubted that his son's excitement was no match for his ambition. Getting Vishnu's strategic and Maurya's operational brain on the project seemed to be a good way for Mahesh to convince his dad to put down the bucks.

The cartel itself expressed some discomfort at watching two of its members diversifying their business interests into new projects, in a world where money equated to power no one wanted one or two of their members gaining more influence than the rest.

Maurya now had to appeal to the next generation in the cartel families to the risk of political climate shifting.

"If we've learned anything over the last few years," he was refereeing to Dhanraj, "is that inactivity is equivalent to degradation. We need to deploy our skills and build from our position of strength to establish our next marker. It is unlikely that we'll keep getting these road development contracts on a platter like before."

When he spoke like a CEO, people listened. The cartel members became equal shareholders into a company that designed their new 21st century territorial model. All the money went in and out of the central organisation set up by Vishnu and Amita. Some of the old cartel members who didn't fancy the rigors of establishing themselves into a new line of business were assigned the responsibility of running the roads, while Maurya and Mahesh operationalised the plan for building the hotels.

It would take five years for the hotel to be completed, by which time Vishnu had reached the ripe old age of seventy-five.

"I've taught you everything that I could have, son." Vishnu's exit from the company was peaceful and emotional, and the reigns of managing their company were passed seamlessly down to Maurya and Amita.

Everyone was happy. Kind of. Maya was halfway through her studies in Paris; Amita was working through the legal labyrinths for permission to build their second, third and fourth hotel. As the hotel's financial success was achieved, Maurya's prediction of them not being able to maintain the road construction monopoly came to pass. The business dried up as paperwork went online and it became much more difficult to make their competitors' tenders vanish. It raised Maurya's stock further in the eyes of his peers.

"Building hotels is taking too long," Maurya mentioned to people around him. "Can't we just buy and refurbish?

It turned out that they could, and the company changed track yet again. They bought a couple of hotels in the country and then in an attempt to test his reach in the world, Maurya went ahead and brought a run-down heritage site in Paris. Needless to say, Maya was never far from his mind, and he was still dreaming of bringing his family together for the third time.

"We are an international company now; you must be happy with everything you've achieved?" One of the cartel leaders had asked him then.

"Moderately happy."

"What's next?"

"This may sound a little preposterous," he smiled ruefully, "but I want to build a city. Think of it as a hotel the size of a city, a paradise on earth. Casinos, golf courses, shopping malls, hospitals... hell, I want that hotel city to have a football club of our own to cheer for in national leagues. It would have everything that you have ever imagined doing in a year of living in a city, all combined together into a hotel that you can check into but never want to leave."

"You want to build Hotel California?" one of the men in the party joked and the others laughed, "You are insatiable, Maurya."

"I am," he said. "I want to buy a little island and build a dream." Everyone sobered up once they realised that he wasn't joking.

"That would take a lot of money."

He had done the math. It would cost ten times more than everything he had amassed until that point. Quite unfortunately for him, the cartel itself was maxed out and cash wasn't quite so easily available anymore. The markets were no longer as bullish as they had been when he had started out, and while money from foreign investors to invest in India had been easy to find, it was a much harder deal to gather capital from Indian investors who wanted to invest overseas.

Amita found a part of the answer eventually, "All those politicians who we have been paying off for years, let's get back all the cash that they've stuffed in their walls and take it with us to build paradise city."

"You mean we launder their money," Maurya half joked, "that's not exactly legal."

"On the contrary, it is no more or less legal than what we've been doing so far."

Maurya laughed. "But how would we even do this?"

Maurya called Vishnu to test the idea with him. "Money laundering investment fund sounds like a grand idea," he joked, "especially if we can take some of that cartel money back from those guys and put it into our business."

"More than what we've given them, we can also take away some of what they've gathered from the other folks over the years."

"Is it going to be enough?" Vishnu asked.

"We don't need the complete capital in equity, as long as we can come to the table with substantial cash, we have enough connections within financial services to get the rest sanctioned in loans."

"Sounds like a heavy investment on a dream, Maurya. You could lose everything that you've earned so far, and more. The people you are talking about are hardly kind investors; this is a pit of vipers that you are stepping into."

"This market in India is volatile, it can go away in a minute. We have a business model that has succeeded so far. We skirt on the edge of law to get things done faster and better. Over the last decade we've seen it work, as long as we can offer what the competition can't. Wherever the competition is stronger, we'll pull them backwards."

"Where are you thinking of building the city?"

"I've checked out a small island right off the coast of West Europe. It is largely uninhabited so far. Asia has it's Macau, US has Vegas, Europe is ready for its crown jewel."

"The administration works a little differently there. Plus, we don't have the same kind of political clout."

"We'll have to build the political clout, and I do feel that the administration is similar enough in just the right ways for us to operate. But I concede your bigger point and promise to not make any rash investments until we have a solid plan of action in place."

Vishnu gave in and came out of retirement to help Maurya work out finances. His primary job was pitching to the political connections.

***

Over recent years, Boy's job description had changed quite a bit as they had made their peace with the cartel and pushed Dhanraj out. He was now the primary enforcer, ensuring that peace within the worker communities was well-maintained and any outside interventions from unnecessarily honest administrative workers or new players were handled adequately, without much friction reaching Maurya.

Maurya tasked Boy now with executing the movement of the finances between India and Europe.

Vishnu's job was a hard sell to begin with, but eventually, the money started to pour in.

Amita had to create a near impossible to crack network of thousands of shell companies till the point that every trace of ownership was lost in a myriad of paperwork, and hard clean cash emerged on the other side that was ready to be invested in the city.

But after all was said and done, they were still well short of what they needed.

Maurya had developed a keen understanding that when one door closed, another tended to open. This final door opened when Maurya found that, unbeknownst to the cartel, Mahesh had been trying to set up a distribution ring for party drugs out of their hotels.

An urgent meeting was called where Mahesh pleaded his innocence but was duly berated and banished from the business.

"I understand where you are coming from, Maurya," the cartel head had said, "but this isn't an easy market to work in if we make too many enemies."

"Who said anything about making enemies? I want Mahesh out because he has mismanaged this and put us under unnecessary risk to make a few quick bucks on the cartel's expense. We will execute this professionally from now on and operationalise it."

The cartel realised that any misgivings that they now had were too late to act on. They had come a long way from the days where a gentle bribe here and there was enough to keep their coffers full and appetites satiated. Greed had given birth to the insatiable beast called Maurya, who had progressively turned them into an extremely efficient criminal enterprise. He sat at the centre of all the money and controlled the armies.

Maurya had reason to be happy with the outcome, for now the final piece of the puzzle had fallen in place for him. He now had a new source of income, not to mention that his new business partners could help in building influence in his new playground.

All the pieces were on the board, "Your dream is finally being realised." They asked him, "You must be a happy man?"

"Moderately happy," he said, perhaps because he knew what the others only suspected. There was more to come.

Book VI

32
Boy

Paradise City
July, 2008

We had a ritual – every time Maurya bought one of my paintings, he asked me to do something difficult for him. Not necessarily difficult to execute, though it usually was, but difficult to live with.

He'd take the painting as a visible symbol of his guilt and then place it somewhere around the house, in his gallery of shame. In a way, he managed to isolate his guilt into a frame, away from his mind and body and close enough to observe at leisure. His fingers traced across the curves of the colours – slowly, surely, deftly he felt the orange and the red, as if channelling his infernal heat towards the canvas.

"The blend is impeccable, Boy" he said without looking up, "little waves of pleasure and little waves of pain, all blended together into one canvas. But what I like the most is how you've not tried to hide one from the other. It's unabashed, it's almost brazen."

Art is subjective, they've often said. One person doesn't always see what another draws. To capture the essence of the art, you needed to know the artist, perhaps not intimately.

He turned towards me, "What was the meaning as you saw it?"

"Insatiable desire – thirsty, all-consuming and ecstatically painful."

"Desire for what?"

I paused, "Everything and nothing, if that makes sense. Every minute of our existence oscillates between an everything and a nothing; a desire to make those ends meet and reach an understanding that while nothing might matter, everything does matter."

"Sounds like a mad quest."

"It is. We are all mad. Why else would we go on living in this insane world?"

"The world isn't insane. The people who question it are."

We paused at that for a few loaded moments. "I want you to get rid of the boy," he said.

I had seen it coming, he seldom brought me down to talk about life.

"Hang the painting somewhere that I can see it every day. A place worthy of the betrayal that it'll represent."

"It'll be done," I nodded. "Questioning the world as it exists isn't insane, Maurya."

"It's pointless, and indulgence in pointlessness speaks of madness to me. You'll be so much better off if you just lived for a dream."

"We have to agree to disagree then. I know you've found your answer in action. Constantly growing, constantly improving. But growing to what end?"

"It ends when life stops. To grow is to exist, Boy. Growth is the only meaningful form of digression. The only one that allows you to feel fulfilled."

"Descartes said, I think therefore I am," I answered him.

"To think is to extend your awareness, it is but one form of growth."

"I have chosen to digress in thought. And I've found true joy there in the form of freedom from ignorance."

"And what has spawned from that?"

I laughed, "More questions unfortunately."

"Sounds like a different kind of ignorance to me." Maurya said, "Is that how all thought into existence must end? Standing at the edge of an endless ocean, staring into the nothingness, thinking that you are looking at the face of god, only to completely miss that fact that there is no god, there are no hidden answers. All the time you had to turn around and look into a mirror and that is it – you. That is the question, and the answer. You."

"We live to live. We need to be insatiable in this quest. To live well perhaps by some definition, as well as possible as much as possible, to take what comes and heroically squeeze the life out of it, into yourself, growing more with every drop. But then, who am I to question you? Do what you will, but kill the boy."

"It shall be done."

33
Caesar

Paradise City
July, 2008

Have you ever felt debilitating fear? When your body refuses to move?

What do you do? You breathe.

"Jules." A man slid into the booth in front of me. I had seen the man at Maurya's house on occasion. Boy, that is how Amita had referred to him.

I'd be insulting your intelligence if I said that I believed for a minute that Maurya would leave me alone before he was done with me.

After I had failed to open Maya's door, I called for help. The fire department arrived before the ambulance; it took them a few minutes to break down the door.

I ran to satisfy my subservience to my animal instinct, to seek comfort away from danger and put up at least a pretence of a fight for survival. I got into the car with him, he drove fast and soon we were within the protective canopy of the mountains.

"This isn't the direction to Maurya's house?"

The guy next to me was different. He exuded a certain kind of persistent anger, the angled jaw line stuck out proudly, the eyes peered imperiously at the road.

"Vous parlez anglais?"

He turned the dominant eyes down at me. "We'll reach the end of this journey soon enough. Perhaps you can use the time for some introspection."

The words could do nothing to hide the harsh innuendo in his statement. He pulled the car down onto a dirt road and began to slow down. I saw him pull the gun out and the instinct of survival surfaced again. In a movement that must have surprised him, I flipped the door open and unspectacularly fell out of the slowing car.

Debilitating fear. You watch because you can't move. Your body stops processing the responses. The mind refuses to function. The instinct to surrender tussles with the need to keep breathing. This tussle could last anywhere between a few seconds and a few minutes, which could mean the difference between life and death.

I pushed myself away from the ground into the forest.

Heat burst through my right leg and pushed me violently to the ground as the bullet struck home.

I heard him moving through the underbrush towards me and instinctively pulled myself in the other direction, my dead leg drawing my weight down.

He came to stand on top of me and levelled the gun on my head.

No one would have been more surprised than me at the resistance my body put up at that moment. Before he had pulled me into the car, I was ready to give up. Had he put me in front of Maurya, I would undoubtedly have infuriated the man further with a vain insulting comment, giving him more reasons to kill me than he had already. But this adventure into the underbrush of the Riviera brought up a rush of adrenaline that had overpowered my self-pity for a few moments.

"Aren't you the artist? Isn't that all your paintings in his library? I wouldn't have thought of you as much of a killer?" I was rambling.

Was that a gentle lapping of water that I heard? I put all the energy in my body into a roll to the side as the gun flashed behind me. I tasted dirt that was thrown upward by the bullet that missed me, only because of my fortuitous move in the other direction. I pushed myself off the ground before Boy could raise the gun again, and then jumped through the air towards the distant sound of the water.

Years of metaphorically jumping off cliffs had done nothing to prepare me for the fall off a real one.

34
Caesar

Outskirts of Paradise City
July, 2008

Keep my back straight and body loose, pushing the water downward with the hands and cycle the legs. The swimming lessons came roaring back to me. But we had never practiced with me using only one leg.

What would the artist do now? Surely jumping in behind me wasn't a practical option? Though who's to know what men who went around shooting people found practical?

The river broke out near the road some distance ahead.

I struggled against the water to get to the edge and slowly pulled myself upwards on the bank. A wave of exhaustion took over me as I finally crawled out of the water onto solid ground. It had been easy to float forward for a while, but now that I had taken a moment to breathe, all the pain from the wound came crashing down on me.

All learning in life should be probability weighted. Why don't we ever train on skills such as stemming blood flow from a gunshot wound? I'd give it to you that it is unlikely to happen to most people, but if it ever did, you probably did not have a margin for error.

For instance, did you tie a knot above or below the wound? Right on top seemed to make sense, so I tore off a shirt sleeve and did that. Easy peasy, what came next? I was wet, cold, and bloody.

I took stock of the situation. I had some wet notes of money, and one leg to run on. Hitching a ride was probably my only option out of there, but the state I was in couldn't possibly inspire confidence in passing cars. The fact that any moment now, the artist could be coming along the road stirred me into action.

I saw a car approaching and stepped out of the shadows and waved my arms. I stumbled a little and fell on one knee as the lights fell on me. The car screeched to a halt a few metres away. A man stepped out and ran the little remaining distance to me.

"Are you ok, young man?"

I shook my head, "I've had a little accident."

"We should get you to a doctor?"

A woman had stepped out of the passenger side, and she moved forward to help.

"Oh *mon dieu*, what happened?"

I heard my words slur, "I somehow managed to shoot myself. Nothing to worry about, as long as we manage to get the bullet out at some point soon."

They piled me into the back of the car and began driving with some urgency, "Don't worry son, we'll take you to a hospital in Paradise City. It's only an hour's ride away down the road."

Cognition stirred at the words. "I can't go to Paradise City, or to any public hospital. I was hunting deer in the forest, considering that it is illegal to hunt here I'm likely to head straight from a hospital to jail."

"It still has to be better than dying," he said. "Why were you hunting deer anyway?"

My back story was beginning to fall apart fairly quickly.

"I'm a hermit, sir. Part time. I'm doing a social experiment, on how to survive from the land."

"With an illegal gun?"

"Mere happenstance. I stumbled upon this ruddy piece of equipment. Gotta curse the old hag that sold it to me. Surely you understand, though now I'm in a pickle, if you take me to a hospital, it'll undoubtedly get noticed and my adventures might be brought to the attention of less understanding folks unlike yourself."

The man looked over the seat of the car. "You need professional help, son."

Blood seeping all over his back seat probably didn't help my argument. "Of course, you are right. It appears that you were heading across the border, if I'm not wrong? Do you think there might be a more easy-going medical practitioner somewhere in the vicinity of where you are headed?"

The couple exchanged a glance. "Well, I suppose we could get our horse doctor look at you. He doesn't have many human patients though, but he is as good at tying up gashes and cuts."

"Beyond kind, sir. You must forgive my poor conversation skills. I'm a little dizzy from all the blood loss."

The conversation took the last bit of energy out of me, and I allowed myself to fall backward.

35
Caesar

Coastal city in North-West Italy
July, 2009

I moved out from the house of a drug lord into the house of a farmer, because, yes, the old couple who rescued me from the road took me in. Life works out like that sometime. Their horse doctor had been sceptical at my story, but Don Fichera was a respected man in the area and the doctor took my word for his.

We were in a small coastal town by the sea where the sun was bright, the sea was a glorious golden blue, and the coffee smelled of home. The easiness of the surroundings did not mean that the circumstances of my landing there were lost on me. The artist could still be looking. Never once in all those moments of longing for Amita and the seduction of Maya, had I stopped to think of how the situation might turn out.

Perhaps at least some part of this had been my fault? But would you have done anything differently in the situation? Could you have staved off Maya when she came at you? Could you have pulled yourself away from Amita when the opportunity presented itself? Would you not have soaked yourself in the pleasures of the Paradise City if you'd been presented with the keys to the bar and a blank cheque book to boot?

Back in the small Italian village, I had been moved to a guest bedroom on the lower floor so that it was easy for me to move around. I developed a taste for Mama Fichera's lasagne very quickly, and Don Fichera's grappa. Both of which turned out to be very delectable to my palate.

"What drove you into the forest boy?" the Don asked me one evening.

A man with a gun was my first thought.

"Nothing much. I was constantly running and just wanted to simplify my life for a bit, so I went to live in the forest for a little while."

"Because switching off your internet wasn't enough?"

"I tried it and it didn't really work."

Don Fichera was a thoughtful man and he left me alone for the most part. I ate the lasagne, drank the local grappa, and watched the horses as I healed.

"Over the years, I've found that wanting less helps me remain calm," the Don said to me a few afternoons later.

By this time, I had forgotten my accidental choice of a philosophical pursuit.

"I'm telling you this because you decided to run off into the forest. To each his own I'd say," Don Fichera continued. "I do what I love all day. I like the honest work of the farm. I have three shirts and three trousers, and a Sunday suit for special occasions for when Mama Fichera likes to go out.

This was an exaggeration; the only time Mama Fichera could go out was when she and the Don went down to the only pub in town for a glass of red wine once a month. Their household was as simple as the people living there. The walls had one picture frame of a son who lived in Milano, the furniture was bare minimum, no flowerpots to put flowers in, and no fancy or un-fancy show pieces. A simple kitchen with a good pair of knives and a practical set of plates, where Mama Fichera would make a simple meal around midday, and we would eat it for lunch and dinner. They spent most of their mornings working around the farm, and most of their afternoons and evenings reading a simple book.

I became comfortable there. It was nice to live off the grid for a bit. My phone had died in the river that night when I was running from the artist. There was a phone in the house which the Fichera's asked me to use to call friends if I liked, but I couldn't think of a friend worth calling. I had no belongings of my own. I was a man free to walk away from things whenever I liked, and I enjoyed that freedom.

"Listen son," Don Fichera said to me one evening. "You are welcome to stay here if you like. I can see that it is serving you well. You were a gangly pale boy when you first got here and now you look like a proper man with colour in your face, now that you've had some decent food inside you. But if you want to stay here, you need to help around the farm. I wouldn't have let a sick boy work, but it'll do you good to turn some of that lasagne into some hard-worn muscles."

I had been refraining from using the ATM machine for a while. The carefully dried few hundred euros I possessed from my past life had been running out and this presented itself as an opportunity to establish a new balance in my life, so I took it.

It was a fun house, all said. They were good natured people, always smiling. "I'm content with having nothing, that means I have everything I need," he replied when I commented on it and then went back about the farm busily.

There was one bar in town, and it was run by an attractive Italian woman, a little further along in age than I, maybe ten years older. Birgitte was curvy in all the right ways and wore red like it was meant to be worn, brazenly. Every few evenings, she'd throw in a shot of grappa at me, and I'd cheer to her health and beauty. We got along just fine.

Mama Fichera had convinced me to buy another shirt with my small savings from my new job. Now I had two, which I could alternate from day to day. Life moved along simple and well, first six months then twelve, a year and then two.

Birgitta convinced me to buy a third shirt in my third year there. She wanted to supplement it with a handy linen jacket that I could wear to the parties on the docks, but keeping in line with Papa Fichera's philosophy, that is where I drew the line.

One day I took a piece of paper to list everything I'd managed to lose. I put Maurya's name on the top, and then added Amita in smaller letters, the killer artist came next. What I'd found was a passionate woman, three clean shirts, Papa Fichera's jovial calmness and Mama Fichera's lasagne. I had also found the sun and the glowing emeralds of sunlight on the water. Funnily enough, they had been there all the time and yet I'd never looked. In all likelihood, I'd stop noticing them again after a while. But I could enjoy it all while the feeling lasted. A thought pushed at the edge of my mind, and I scribbled my name under the mad artist's. I'd finally managed to escape from myself.

36
Caesar

Milano
July, 2009

The trip to Milano was supposed to be routine. We'd drive down with Mama Fichera, pick up some things for the farm and then drive back the same evening. Milano combined both old rustic charm with new age glitz. Mama Fichera was spending some time with her son and grandchildren, which gave me the opportunity to explore the city.

I walked past the Duomo into a wide street. Birgitte liked fine things, especially if they were red. Maybe I could get her a gift, something we could both enjoy, such as some of that lingerie from Agent Provocateur.

The problem arose when the cash fell short. I had gone for over two years without touching one of my credit cards. There was a slim chance that anyone was monitoring my statements, but lacy underwear seemed to be a poor reason to reattach a thread with my old life.

Mama Fichera was a fine woman, dutiful, content, and easy to be around. In the two years of knowing them, I had never seen her complain, though she couldn't help but let this wistfulness come over her sometimes. If only Papa Fichera had given her some nice lingerie from time to time. Birgitta would have been delighted to get the present and I could already think of ways in which she could have gone on to thank me.

I hadn't played Poker for a while, but a short game to double the money could be enough to get me past the cashier at the lingerie store. Maybe I could also throw in the pearl necklace.

The place was empty when I entered, not many people played poker in the middle of the day here. Birgitte would have to do without her present. Anyway, Papa Fichera would have been angry at the thought of putting the idea of luxury into a village girl's head. "Every time she'll put it on, she'll be sad," he would have said, "for the life she wasn't living."

Life seamlessly fit back into the way it was in a matter of days. The little casino in the basement of the mall seemed to be a million lifetimes away. However, perhaps fate had something else in mind. One day, not long after the visit to Milan, I found August waiting for me at Birgitte's pub.

37
Caesar

Coastal city in Northwest Italy
July, 2009

It was a weird feeling to embrace my old best friend. I felt both a familiar exhilaration and a trepidation not unlike a cat caught in the light of an oncoming car.

"I'm fine," I replied.

"You *look* fine, old bloke. Never thought of you as a farm hand."

"How did you find me?"

The expression on August's face wavered. "Straight to the point! Won't you let me buy you a drink first?"

He waved at Birgitte and asked her to pour us two beers. There must have been some discomfort on my face and Birgitte's face mirrored it. August looked between us and then smiled, "I should have known that you'd be sleeping with the prettiest girl in the town."

"How did you find me, August?"

He became uncomfortable at my direct query, but the readiness of his response indicated that he was prepared for it. "Maurya wants you to come back to Paradise City. He has had eyes out for the past two years. You were spotted in a casino in Milano, and someone followed you down to this village from there."

Crippling fear beckoned again like an old friend.

"Look, he could have sent any of his other men to come and get you, but he found me and sent me. He doesn't want to do it like that, he sent you a friend because he wants to set things right," August said.

"And you believe him?" I asked.

"No. But it's either you who pays or me, and considering that you are the one who fucked him over—" his voice trailed off.

How much running is a man capable of? Birgitte observed us from a distance.

"All right," I said.

"What?"

"I'll come to meet him."

Was it relief that I could see on August's face?

"But I have a question."

"Ask me anything," August said.

"Why did you come?"

Uncertainty flashed on his face. "Because I wanted to, I wanted to help you. I couldn't imagine this turning out the wrong way just because you saw an ugly face at the bar."

"Your face doesn't exactly solve that problem."

"You'd know, that's got to be a joke, considering that you wake up every day and look at an uglier version of it in the mirror. Hey lady, do you think we look alike?" he asked Birgitte before turning back to me. Listen, with all due respect to your girlfriend, this place is a little drab. Do you think we can pick up a bottle of some hard stuff here and drink it on the docks or something?"

A few hours later, our reflections looked back at us in the water – friends once, strangers now.

"How have you lived these past few years, August?"

"What do you mean?" He was more relaxed now than earlier in the afternoon. Half a bottle of rum seemed to have done the trick.

"I meant what I said, have you lived well?"

"Well enough, I suppose."

"Have you spent a fair amount of time thinking about life?"

"Me, no, a little, I don't know. Perhaps. It is a dangerous thing, isn't it? Thinking?"

I laughed, "Maybe you are right. For a long time, I felt that I didn't need it, then when I realised that I did, I was afraid to do it for a long time. I was afraid of what I'd find. I used to think that thinking was a losing proposition. An event without an upside in a world where nothing mattered anyway."

"You were always a bit nihilistic."

"A bit, yes."

"But you think differently now?"

"Yes. Now I know that there is a possibility for do-overs in life. The present matters, even if nothing else does. If the present seems to be too onerous, you can go back to the start."

"But wouldn't that mean that you'd lose valuable time?"

"Lose time for what? Where are we going that is more important to be than now? I cannot come to see Maurya. You know what he's going to do. After this drink is done, I'm going to walk away from this place. I'm going to vanish again, I know not where, but far. You'll never see me again. Maurya will never see me again, this I promise."

I should have left a note for Birgitte, maybe I could come back for her one day. That was a lie. I had stopped lying to myself a while ago. It was funny that the moment a tendril of my old life reached out to me, I had fallen into old traps again.

That said, I began to get up, "I would have advised you to not drive while you are drunk, but we don't have a guest house in the village where you'd be welcome. You can finish the rest of the bottle if you like, and then leave." I stumbled slightly. "Maybe I could sit down for a while more to sober up a bit myself."

I put a hand out on my old friend's shoulder, "I'm sorry."

“I’m sorry too,” for the first time that evening there was honesty in August’s expression. “I was afraid you’d act this way.”

“What do you mean?” were the last words I said before slumping forward on the ground.

38
Boy

Coastal city in Northwest Italy
July, 2009

The blood lined the rock.

The boy sat huddled in the corner, hugging his legs, shivering in the warm weather. His haunted eyes had seen me kill his friend. The blood splattered on the rocks made for an interesting pattern, like the pattern life would make when thrown lazily and fruitlessly at the vagaries of time. It was an interesting image, perhaps I could paint it when I got back to my town.

The boy was incoherent by now. I pushed him into the back seat and then began to drive back to the city. He cried and for a moment it felt as if he was choking on his tears.

I opened the back windows to let the cold air in, it did things to you. It reminded you to breathe.

"You did well, August," I said finally. "Maurya would be pleased." He didn't answer.

"We have sent word; the money for your sister's surgery is in your account now."

He nodded. He was lost for a while.

"What did you do with Jules?"

I didn't know how to be careful with my answers. "Somebody will take care of it. He has vanished once before, he'll vanish again, this time for good."

"That's what he said."

"What?"

"That he wanted to vanish."

I remained silent. Who was I to rob a man of his chance to mourn?

"Do you have any place you want to go?" I asked August.

He shook his head, so I drove on towards my home. He could rest on my couch for a few days, some quiet days in the sun and sand would help set him right, it always did.

He was desolate. I knew the feelings all too well. I could almost see melancholy wrap its loving arms around him. Hello old friend. Fortunately for August, melancholy came with an expiry date. The memory will stay with him for a long time, but melancholy itself would move on. There is a promiscuity to melancholy. For no one person can hold on to it, and it doesn't want to hold on to one person.

"I don't want him to vanish," he said before drifting off into silence.

"August?" I began.

"I don't want to be called by that name anymore."

What do you want to be called? I wanted to ask but refrained. There'll be time.

"Just remember the question that you need to find the answer to, '*What would it take to survive – this?*'" I said instead, "Once you have the answer to that, life would fall in line."

Epilogue

August
Europe and South America
August 2015

If it hadn't been for the rock shackled to my legs and the fact that my body was slowly losing strength, I may have managed to stay afloat. The rock, on the other hand, strained at pulling me downwards. It was heavy enough that I would surely sink, light enough that my body would go all the way down, instinctively kicking out for every torturous second.

Before I go, I owe you a few explanations. We were two – his name was Jules, mine was August. People called him Caesar first. He came and conquered everything in sight, but when he was eventually vanquished, killed because of my weakness, I took his name. He was Kinetic where I was Katastematic. He was all about physical pleasures, chasing gratification through instant fulfilment of desires. He lived in the present like no person I'd ever seen. He was thirsty, he set out every day to quench it with alcohol and sex.

I, August, on the other hand, strived to find peace within myself, epicure. I craved it. I narrowed down my desires to something base. Remember the times we spent in Motril with Boy and Victoria. I had nothing, but I wanted nothing, and yet I owned both the sea and sun. It mattered little that I had to share it with a few billion people in the world. Everything I needed and wanted was mine to take. I could boast of being in the presence of some great minds that touched my life –

Schopenhauer and Nietzsche, Goethe and Spinoza. I had them all. Food in my stomach and the occasional dose of alcohol in my blood stream. I was Katastematic.

But you know what happened. Jules wasn't fully kinetic; he desired the peace in spite of having a near endless access to everything he needed to satisfy his kinetic needs. I wasn't fully Katastematic; I desired the physical pleasures denied to me when Victoria was with Boy and that hurt me. There is an important message here that I understand almost too late: you can't have one without the other. The whole concept of pleasure is to balance yourself, in all forms, you need to satisfy the urges and you need to be able to find the peace, one without the other is baseless. He had a chance to find peace with someone and he threw it away. It cost him his life in the end.

I wouldn't claim that I had everything under control, and yet when the time came, I made the right mistakes in life. I stumbled upon Victoria, who proved to be my salvation in the end.

The water pressed into me from all sides. The dark stillness around me brought about a numbing calmness and I did my relentless brain the courtesy of kicking out at the shackles a few last times. The chains began to slide free as I wrested my feet around. I kicked harder and heard the padlock break free. I had earned a favour from Maurya. He had now repaid it through a loosely stuck lock, a flimsily tied chain and a bullet that grazed past my body. One Caesar had died years before, so that another Caesar could live.

I surged upwards and finally broke water. I was unsure of how long it had been, perhaps two minutes or three? The coast was slightly more than a kilometre away and the boat, quite fortunately, was not in sight.

The money that I was supposed to give to Don Camorra was on its way to another account, funnily enough not very far from this place, but the Don would see none of it, hopefully. I swam down the lake for the next twenty minutes and then swam towards the opposite coast from the Don's villa.

Climbing out on the sparse bank after spending close to half an hour in the water was a welcome break. But it had taken every bit of my will power to get this far. A road ran right beside the lake and a house stood on top of a short hill on the other side.

I did a quick check over my wounds; none of them seemed like they'd kill me tonight. The thumb throbbed as if to remind me that it was still broken. Perhaps I could steal some clothes from the house up the hill. But this was still too close to the Don's house. Any news of a suspicious break-in would raise questions that aren't easily answered. And god forbid if they had any stray cameras hanging around. I began to hike down the road and then broke into a jog in an attempt to warm my cold body. An approaching car made me pause my hike and almost a few seconds too late I clumsily ducked behind a tree.

The car slowed down as it approached me. Should I run or should I hide? Where could I run? Back in the lake would probably kill me anyway, the only other option left was to run straight at the car. Perhaps I could take on whoever was in there and then drive away. I looked around for things I could use as a weapon.

A head finally peeped out of the car as the window lowered, and Boy's voice rang out, "Are you enjoying the cold that much? Or would you fancy jumping in so we could get out of here?"

***

The rest, as they say, was simple.

Boy drove me into France and left me in a small southern village a few hundred kilometres from the Andorran border. From Andorra to Madrid, Madrid to Guadeloupe, Guadeloupe to San Juan, San Juan to San Jose, and San Jose to my tiny haven in the middle of nowhere. I used different passports every time I moved.

I spent at least two days in every city as a rule, but always less than four. Every journey carried me farther from my world, every trip carried me closer to Victoria. Till the final boat ride brought me home. She must have seen the boat cutting through the sea because by the time I paid the man for dropping me off, I saw her walking down the steps that we'd carved on the rock from the house to the pier.

She stopped a few feet in front of me. I could feel her eyes caressing the wounds on my body slowly, checking for lasting damage perhaps. A twinkle crept in her eye for she had quickly seen past the physical aberrations and was finally beginning to celebrate my arrival.

Years before she had picked me up from the brothel, and we spent a few weeks moving from place to place trying to find our next haven. No matter where we went, we found it hard to escape the spectre of Boy. In the end, we decided that we had to try to leave the continent, and that is how we ended up in South America. We found another little shack by the sea, but found that it was hard to live in a crumbling house without Boy around to fix it and make it habitable.

Victoria also raised the question of trying out her theory. She was at peace again and wanted to strive for a life where nothing could disturb it.

"Let's find an island, where there's nothing for miles but the sea for company. We could fill the place up with your books." She wanted to build a house that wanted for nothing.

"That's going to take a little money," I said.

"I suppose." We had left it at that for some time, but the thought came back to me over and over again. It took some doing, but here we were now, ready to jump off into our next adventure together.

We were on a tiny island up from the coast of Guatemala that shared its name with the girl I loved, and here we could finally start building our humble abode.

Octavia was Jules's sister. I hoped that she was well now, and that one day she might find the strength to leave the horror of her ordeal behind. Years earlier, Maurya and Boy had put an impossible proposition in front of me. My sister was dying. Maurya offered to pay for her treatment in return of me helping them catch Jules. They had been tracking him for a couple of years and it appeared that finally he had stumbled back on the grid from wherever he had been hiding. I struggled with the choice for days, but eventually I gave in. You know the rest.

Victoria touched my face lightly. "I missed you," she kissed me gently. We'd get past the events of the week past, of that I was sure. We had a hundred million reasons to be joyful.

The story isn't completely over. No story ever is, is it? Shall we ascribe the rest to life and say goodbye. For now, in the very least.

You have my deepest gratitude for making it this far. If life presents an opportunity, we'll meet again. Otherwise, may life fare you well, dear friend. May you find your joy! All of it in its eternal recurrence.

Acknowledgements

I have a lot to be grateful for, and many people to be grateful to.

Thank you Jehanara Wasi for going through the early proofs of the book, and Harini Srinivasan for being the first at challenging my occasional meanderings.

My publicist, guide and friend, Lipika Bhushan – thank you for the thousand or so pieces of advice.

Stuti, Arup and the rest of the Srishti Publishers team, for being honest and trusted critics, and for challenging me to take my storytelling to the next level. I've learnt more about writing in three rounds of editing with you, than in years of writing.

Thanks Mom, for introducing me to the world of metaphors, similes, tragedies, romance, thrillers and fantasies. Without that introduction, I'd never have fallen in love with books, and not a word from me would have fallen on paper.

To the rest of my family, thank you for always being there. For the love, the belief, and the motivation. I'm looking at you, Randev Dad, Koul Dad, Koul Mom, Aditya, Sneh, Anshul, Diya, Geet, Kirti Bhaiya, Sumi Didi, Dikhsu, Anuj and the rest of the Randev and Koul clan.

Thanks also to all my friends and colleagues, who make life fun and interesting. You know who you are, and you know you are the best.

Last, to my best friend and wife, Anshika. Thank you for being my biggest fan and most honest critic. Thank you for being my creative sparring partner, and for being the challenger to all my weak plot points. Thank you also for being my companion on all my adventures. Without those, there would be no stories to tell. You are as much a writer of this book as I.

I started writing this book in my cramped bedroom in the 7th Arrondisement in Paris. The first 30% of the story literally poured itself out on the pages in the first month. Thanks to Paris for giving me the inspirational trigger to write this piece. Long may our love remain.

Love,
Atul